T0118569

AINT NO LOVE IN THIS TOWN

INTENT TO TO DISTRIBUTE IN OAKLAND

WILLIAM P. WARE

ISBN: 978-1-4669-5493-9 (sc)
ISBN: 978-1-4669-5549-3 (e)

Trafford rev. 12/14/2012

 www.trafford.com

North America & international
toll-free: 1 888 232 4444 (USA & Canada)
phone: 250 383 6864 ♦ fax: 812 355 4082

So first and foremost I want to thank god for putting this izzism in me to be able to make things like this come together. I want to thank everybody that believed in me and even the ones that didn't. Real niggas do real things and this is just a prime example. I got an eppiphany one day when I was incarcerated or maybe it was just that the books I was reading in there wasn't none of them from my area. So in an attempt to keep em talking I wrote this book specifically for my loved ones!!So here came "Ain't no love in this town. By William Ware. A dedication to my city . . . Oakland, CA. Been in the bay area all my life. Done seen a lot of shit an prolly gon see a lot more!! Born and raised in Oakland, CA. Attended some berkeley schools and graduated from wyotech fremont with a diploma in automotive technology. I am currently flooding Oakland, CA and surrounding cities with dope ass music videos giving some of the youth an outlet or atleast helping them to get started as a potential talent for the music world.

Please check out my channel on youtube I know you will love it: getmoneyboyyyz tv/youtube.

Shout out to all of the artist that I been workin wit: C.B.I goonz, relly rell, King James, wonni-bo, ant and the cash-out camp.

Shot out all my niggas locked down sittin in that thang keeping it solid!! Functioning on the mainline!!

I also want to give a shot out to roneka tate who gave me a hand with some of the editing and also was a big support with constructive criticism.

I want to give a shout out to every hood in the bay. Never let anybody tell that you can't do it . . . . Cause that's some bullshit!! All my real niggas that rock wit me and sitting on a penny till it turn green.

#Continue to hold post . . . .
#Here come the sunny dayz!!
#Gmb empire!!
#Gmb empire!!
#Gmb empire!!

Now most importantly . . . . "The dedication" . . . . I wanna dedicate this book to:my grandmother, my mother, because with out you I would not be here!! My father Chris Ware R.I.P and Ukiah Ware my oldest daughter yo Daddy love you and I want you to always reach for the stars baby and do whatever you wanna do in life. To my oldest son Trishten and my youngest son Josiah this is for yall!! When you grow up I want you to understand that your Daddy was a master of his craft in whatever he put his mind to, and that's the way that I want you guys to be!!

To my extended family I love yall!! Reach for the stars!!

Anybody I forgot, I love you and reach for the stars!!

#Imma give it all I got!!

Yours truly,
Will 4 real gmb empire
C.E.O and president.

CHP 1
LICK CITY

"Hey Nesse come and check this out!" Nesto whispered. Between two dressers and a night stand they had finally found what they were looking for. "The safe baby!, Yes!", With about four and a half inches hanging out the wall, so shiny Nesto could see the logo from Finesse's rockawear jeans clear as glass. "Come on man grab that side . . . . one! . . . Two! . . . . Three!" After fifteen minutes of ram-shacking the joint looking for valuables, cash, and electronics they finally found the safe. They gathered every molecule of air they had to drag the safe to the car. Man they had a hell of a time running through houses because it always felt like christmas . . . Gifts for free. Little did they know that their greed and addiction to money, cars, clothes, and hoes would make it a long summer. After two long blocks, a left then a right . . . They ran right into the dick heads. "Hit'em nigga, we out!!!" Nesto screamed. With the adrenaline rushing, all they could think about was what corners to cut because they wasn't going back. The rearview had a clear vision of what they called "cherries and blueberries" which was just slang for police lights. Nesse had his foot on the pedal so hard that it almost bust through the floor. With a car full of stolen shit, giving up was not an option, so . . . . Wasn't no stopping them now. Nesto and Nesse were weaving in and out of lanes, this was the real "midnight club". They had to be doing about 100 miles per hour. "Oh shit!! Five-o!!" Nesse yelled as he tried to turn the wheel, then they heard a loud "smack" as they got clipped from the right passenger side by a police car. All the rollers in that area got a call to seal up the perimeter when the silent alarm triggered the police at the eastmont sub-station. After they finally got out the hills, 8 miles and two lights later, they were sitting in the intersection unconscious with two free phone calls waiting at north county before their transfer to santa rita. Nesto had seen this picture oh too many times before . . . . County yellows & blues and anticipating pod time was not a good look for them. When they woke up . . . They were back in the box . . .

CHP 2
BACK IN THE BOX

After a good eight hours they had them on the bus to santa rita. That was the "big house as far as the county was concerned. The inside of the bus looked like a jail on wheels, with all the cubicles and steel gates it had in it.

Very seldom did they send a co-ed group on the bus, but on this trip, they lucked up and ran into one of the slickest, hood rich sistahs, that they would definitely cross paths with again before it was all over with. Her name was "Lola" but they called her "Lollipop" because you could never catch her without a sucker in her mouth. Nesto went to school with her, since junior high and that's how he knew her real good. Lollipop was on her way back from a court date for a probation violation for" running them sliders" that's slang for credit card fraud. She definitely was the bitch to see on the streetz, cuz the hustles she always had, complimented the saying of "if it don't make dollars, then it don't make cents!! "Nesto looked over the crowd of men on the bus, a majority of black african males. He thought to himself that the government got a smooth operation going with a bus full of lab rats. "Hey Lollipop . . . . You know they just knocked me and ness" Nesto said trying to talk over all the noise on the bus that sounded like a cafeteria full of hungry kids. "Shit nigga you know they be trying to be on erythang . . . ." "Yea, big brothers always watching" she said shaking her head . . . "Shit we had made it out and was whipping corners den next thing we know, one time had they bumpers all on our shit!" Nesto said briefly running it back to Lollipop about how it all went down. "Ay you still out there in the west or what?" Lollipop asked. "Shit I just barely slide through now, you know shit aint the same." Nesto said "true" Lollipop followed in agreement. "Nesto and ness had this trap house in East Oakland on "tha fruit" short for "Fruitvale St." This was a house that was usually abandoned by its owners because of foreclosure and took over by local drug dealers to sell drugs out of. This was where Nesto and Nesse spent most of their time. "Ay Nesto, I remember you use to be on my line, like you really wanted to fuck with a bitch but . . . . , I cant "slow down" I move to fast on the gas don't chase me" she rapped from a song that was playing on the radio and pleading her case at the same time. The radio station mustve been on 106.1 Kmel, cuz they were the ones that always aired the local talent. "You a supersnot bopper" Finesse grawled "you know we only fuck wit top notch bitches" letting his presence be known. "Shit I bet yall gone feel me when ya see me on the outs, cuz I know im a dimepiece!" Lollipop said convincing herself. "Lollipop . . . He just talking shit . . . Besides, you know how I get down" Nesto said. "My pfn number is "bdf510" "so send me a kite with yo info on it so I can hook up with you on the outs, so me and my niggas can get this gmb shit moving mean out here!!" Nesto said all excited. "Dats real!" Lollipop murmered blushing at the chicken heads tuned in to her show. "You still my bitch girl, I got dumb love for you . . . Remember dat!" Nesto said. After they made it through the out skirts of the city, they finally made it to the santa rita facility where they would ride out the rest of their time unless they didn't beat the case and ended up in the state pen. Coming to ritas house you were guaranteed to see one of yo niggas from every hood. That shit was krazy. When ness and Nesto got off the bus, they seperated the new books from the inmates that were already dressed out in county clothes and were just returning for court. Touching down in that mutha fucka was a real process. Some were happy that they were going home, and the rest were sad faces. Mostly youngstas fighting murder beefs, car jacking charges and shit like that. They moved through about four different multi-purpose rooms before they actually got to dress out. Imagine 50 niggas in one room dressing and undressing, handing their street clothes to an officer in exchange for their county jumpsuits. They were there another fourty-five minutes before the co's came to take everybody to their designated housing areas. "Rodriguez! Stone! Jenkins! Laprince! . . . . "Yellows!" The C.O yelled rounding up his first group. Nesto gave ness a head bob to let em know that was his train. Ness nodded back. "Jackson! Ellison! Gomez! and Pierr! . . . . "Blues!" The C.O shouted. They had split them up just as Nesto had expected all along. Nesto was going to yellows which was a maximum security unit with two man cells. Nesse was going to the "thunder dome" so they called it, because it was something like a fight club. Shit was always goin on in that thang. The thunder dome was like dorm living or old fashioned army barracks and everybody wore blue jumpsuits. It looked like a big ass group home over there. "Damn . . . They splittn us up" Finesse said, as he slid Nesto a piece of cardboard from his lunchpack that had numbers on it. "Use these! . . . I put my baby momma's address on here too . . . "So if you need to send a kite out, send it to her and she gone make it happen for you". Nesse finished, just as Nesto retrieved the information from him, the co's came to take the first group to the dorms. And just like that, Finesse was gone. Nesto didn't worry about Nesse because in good faith he knew that he would hold his own. It might have been a whole 3hrs before they came and got nestos group. When Nesto made it to unit 22 east, he seen a lot of familiar faces. When he got in they were out for pod time. That was kool because he needed to use the phone to make some phone calls. As soon as he picked up the phone he got approached by three goonz. "You from frisco?" One asked inquiring if he was from a certain area. "Nah . . . The town!" Nesto rebuttled with great anger. "Well . . . . The "town" phone is over there!" The other punk said and pointed way across the pod. By the time Nesto got to the other phone he got approached again. "Ay lil homie . . . . You affiliated?" Popping his knuckles, the shaquil oneil looking nigga asked inquiring if he was a part of a well known prison group . . . "Nah . . . civilian!" He snarled as he noticed the invisible chains attached to the phones and fell back so he could peep game and check play. He was surrounded by a secret society of niggas who wanted to belong to something or used the brotherhood as a shield or source of protection. Niggas like Finesse and Nesto felt they didn't need to join no umbrella because they had too many friends already, that were knee-deep underneath. One thing about the street politics was, it really made a difference who you were and who you knew. On the right street with the wrong license could cost you out there. Not only did Nesto and Finesse have many friends affiliated, but Nesto got a lot of love when they found out who his brother was. His big brother "dollar" had been in and out of the system his whole life. He held rank with that "love." Dollar was the nigga on the block that made everybody laugh, he was hella crazy but with a heroin addiction, every time you turned around, that nigga was on a lick trying to feed his habit. When dollar got indicted in a murder from across the water, Nesto knew that the chances were real slim that he'd ever see his brother on the streets again. He might have had some get back, if they didn't put that "l" for "life" on it. That "l" will have you rotting in the joint, real talk! Believe it or not though, Nesto would rather do state time than county time anyday. Point blank, county time was harder time. In the state pen he felt like he had more coming to him and he could do his time with a little more leisure. Anything you could get on the street, was the same shit you could get in the joint. You'd be amazed.

After Nesto checked in and went through the whole "who are you?, And who you know thing?" He was making calls on everybody's phones. For the first week all he came out of his cell to do was use the phone. He didn't wanna play dominoes, spades, pinocle, or none of that shit. He had everything that meant anything to him out there on the streets and he wasn't trying to make that shit-hole like home. Being that they only let one half of the pod out at one time, he still didn't really know if he had any of his goonz from the streets in there with him. By the time he got his door closed for lockdown, he barely had time to re-organize his desk, that was molded into the wall with a couple of magazines occupying it. There must've been every niggas hood tagged on the wall, niggas really felt the urge to leave their marks. It's just the way it was. "Nesto wasssup bruh?? What you doing here?" A grimey deep voice yelled through the crack of his cell, "the same thing you doing here . . . Only different charges" . . . Nesto fired back, laughing at his own joke. It was "Stackz". He was Nesto's homie from the group home. They were from the same hood, the killa twenties and had some of the same acquaintances. "Damn, what you doing in here Stackz?"

Nesto asked a hundred percent curious. "They said I tried to rob that gas station on 34th and san pablo across the street from the california hotel, nigga can you believe that??" Stackz said trying to convince himself he was inocent. He looked at Nesto, Nesto looked right back at him, and they both just busted out laughing cuz they both knew that he was full of shit. "Fuck you Nesto, I aint do shit!" Stackz said grimmacely laughing. "They aint got nothing on me, I'll be out soon!" It was something about the way Stackz said it, that didn't sit right with Nesto but he couldn't quite put his finger on it. Yet . . . he told Stackz about the shit that he and ness had just got into. The silence grew loud between them for a couple of minutes then Stackz got called down to the card table. "Ay bruh, if you need anything im in rm 2. I see you already got phone action already but if you need some more let me know" Stackz said. "Oh yea and now

I got that phone over there so, start using that one too." Nesto realized right then and there that Stackz was affiliated with those secret society groups. Nesto didn't have a problem with it, as long as he didn't try to pull him in too. But little did Nesto know, accepting that offer, got him plugged into the equation without even knowing it. Shit was crazy like that sometime. "So when I aint on it, make sure like hell that you are aight?" Stackz said. "And if anybody say sumthin to you about the phone let me know." Stackz said with a serious mugg on his face. Nesto gave him a pound through the glass and Stackz was gone. Nesto wasn't new to this jail lifestyle at all, as a matter of fact, it was like dejavu. Nesto knew exactly what to do. Tomorrow there would be a new triumph, that phone now belonged to Nesto and anybody else associated wit gmb. Nesto kept the tradition. If you wasn't connected you wouldn't be reaching out and touching nobody from his phone. By the time the next day swung around, Nesto had a locker full of goodies, all the writing materials he needed and not to mention enough hygiene stuff to last him about two years. He made sure the niggas who rode wit him was taken care of. He had a nigga from every hood in Oakland with him. A couple of niggas from the east, a couple from the west, a hand full of polar bears from the north and chosen few that he had went to school with in b-town. Nesto had put together an all-star line up. He had about a hundred more dollars worth of shit coming from letting niggas use the phone. They took turns holding that phone down, shit when it came down to it they were pullin revenue straight through that muthafucka. Nestos's court date came by before he knew it. All he could do the day before court is get well rested because he knew those court days were really long days. A long ass day of listening to everybodies lies about how they was getting money on the outs. Every nigga wanted to be a pimp or a rapper, and hearing half the stories these cats told, always made Nesto real irritated by the days end. Nesto got up off the cot when he heard his name screetch over the intercom. "La prince! Wake up! Court!" . . . . The intercom blared loudly. Nesto got up and washed his face and got his cup of coffee ready. He cut the bottom out of his socks, so he could use them as sleeves and got ready for the door to pop for breakfast. Nesto already had some oatmeal in a cup, ready to get it in. All he needed was some hot water. Nesto hardly ever ate the county food cuz that shit just ran straight through him. He believed in eating meals that were made for champions. This mornings special was "shit on a shingle" another example of why Nesto finned for himself in there instead of relying on the county. They moved Nesto through three multi-purpose rooms after breakfast, and by the time they got to the fourth room Nesto seen Finesse kicked back against the wall drinkin a cup of coffee watchin the news. "Bruh wassup wit it!!" Nesto said "you ready to get this shit over wit?". Nesto had been around the block enough times to know that today was just an arraignment, and they were going to step in to get their charges and a new court date to show up in court. After the long ass day Nesto had already anticipated, passed at court, he finally made it back to his bed. Just like he thought. Today was nothing more than arraignment and their next court date wasn't for another couple of weeks. The pod worker came and slid a note under his door and did it moving too fast to follow with questions. It was a note from "Poppa". He was the next in charge in the chain of command. It turned out that some niggas tried to get jazzy with him over the phone. The word was that, it wasn't over. Thats just the way it was, things had to be resolved A.S.A.P . . . So he got two bars of soap, put them in a sock and sat it on the table for the morning. When the a.m came around Nesto got up a little earlier than usual and started his program. He was standing in front of his bunk with the makeshift weapon wrapped around his hands and as soon as the door popped for breakfast, just as he had suspected, he had two unwanted guest waiting outside. Nesto swung the soap in the sock like drunken nun-chuks. When he hit the first oversized punk, he tried to take his whole damn jaw off. All you heard was them niggas going rounds from the outside of that cell. It sounded like somebody was slapping ground beef up against the wall. When Nesto got done handling his business, he shouted "I wake up the same time every morning so, if you wanna run it back you know where im at" as he stepped right over them to go and join everybody else for breakfast. The punks got themselves together and came out of the cell like nothing ever happened. Shit was crazy. Nesto headed to get some hot water for his coffee. The pod was silent and everybody knew what time it was. It was all about respect. As he put the hot water in his cup, an alarm sounded so everybody start locking down and return to their cells. The co's popped the doors for the top tiers, so he seen Poppa step out. Nesto raised both of his arms over his head to form an "x" he had just let Poppa know that he had taken care of the situation. When the next pod time came, Nesto took his time getting to the phone. He wanted somebody, dared anybody, for the fact of the matter, to touch that phone. He wanted someone who had no business with it, to step up so he could get another adrenaline rush. For the rest of the time that Nesto had in 22 east, he had no problems over the phone. Today he stayed on the phone all day and didn't let anybody use it. He saw the look of anger coming from a variety of different faces so he knew he upset somebody, he didn't care though. Whoever sent them bum ass niggas to try and ride was mad as fuck about the lack of control they had over a real nigga. Nesto called a couple of chicken heads to come visit, cracked a couple of jokes, lined up some money for more commisary and then it was time to lock it down again. He spent a lot of days like this, it really began to become a program for him because it helped him pass the time. At 6:00 am they had chow, then he went back to sleep until morning pod time. During morning pod, him and the squad spent time conditioning: push ups, pull ups, burpies, and dips. Just in case it ever popped off again, they'd be ready. Working out was mandatory, because you just never knew when it was gone pop on some shady shit. After morning pod, he always went back to the room and made a big spread before returning back to sleep. Spreads were like a real ghetto feast working with anything you got. In other words, it was the closest that you were going to get to something that came out of a restaurant especially in rita's house. Nesto had been in and out of the system so damn much that his spreads were draped with top of the line ingredients: noodles, oysters, mayo, and hot chips. Everybody used different chips, but Nesto liked the hot cheetos because it give it that spicy effect. By the time he finished cooking it was time to go out and get the county meal. Even tho Nesto had a locker full of food he still went to go collect what was his, so he could barter with it. After lunch, he layed back on his rack and flipped open a book he had been reading. The book was called "behold of the pale white horse" he liked reading books like this because even though he was a thug, he was on a journey in search of the truth. Besides, he had read all the terri woods, donald goines, chunichi's and any other urban fiction publications they had. He would do all the reading that he could before he fell asleep. They had chow at about 5 o'clock and then came out at night pod at about 7 o'clock. All the inmates looked forward to pod time. It made them feel free inside of their imprisonment. Some wanted to watch T.V, some wanted to play games, everybody had a different outlet for freedom. "Freedom? . . . Yea right!" Nesto thought about how sometimes they took pod time away when they were having problems in that unit. After pod time Nesto did a little bit of reading until he fell asleep. That was pretty much his program while he was down. Shit when he woke up the next day, it had been six months fighting this case. The court was holding them for 1 count of residential burglary, conspiracy, possession of stolen property, and evading the police. Well atleast they put a retainer fee down on a really good lawyer. He was known for getting niggas off on some wild shit ya feel me?? He also helped a lot of niggas get their "rider money" this was basically when victims got compensated for getting beat up by the Oakland police. The attorney's name was j. Mcdagger. It was the third of the month and they had another court date tomorrow. "(Chanting)na . . . . Na . . . . Nah . . . Na . . . . Ey . . . Hey . . . Ey . . . Gooodbye!" (Chanting)(music ends).

You could hear the sound of somebody's player card getting revoked. There's a 90% chance that someone had just got their face smashed in and rolled up out of the unit. It was just crazy laughter. Sounded like a cafteria full of hungry kids again. Some of the things that happen was like a reality tv episode. You were basically considered a bitch if you got beat up and somebody made you leave. He slept through the rest of the time they had to themselves when they wasn't programming. Finesse layed in his bed motionless plotting his return. Nesto did the same. He thought about the mistakes that he would not make again. After that, he faded to black. When he woke up the next day it was from the horn of the intercom. "Laprince! . . . . Court! . . . Get up for court in ten minutes!!" Nesto got up and put together a super black cup of coffee, with no creamer and no sugar. When the doors popped . . . . He was outta there. Nesto hit up all of his potna's doors so he could shoot the shit for a min. He made Stackz the last stop. "Ay what's poppin Stackz? . . . Dis might be the last one" Nesto said. "That's kool bruh" Stackz said as he gave Nesto a dap handshake. "Im be in this bitch fighting this shit till they throw me something good" Stackz said. "Well if everything goes as planned today, I can put you on wit my manz and he can get you out dis hell hole aight?" Nesto promised. "Everybody for court!" The co screamed out over the intercom "aight bruh, wish me luck!" Nesto said. And then he was gone. "Good luck bruh!!" Nesto heard Stackz yell from his cell before he got through the unit door. When Nesto hit the yard, the breathe of fresh air took his mind on a trip. He could not wait to get back to the real world and push play. Nesto had gained about 26 plbs. Since he's been down in the facility. Face looking fatter and like two shades lighter than usual. "It's time to let us go" Nesto thought to himself. Finesse and Nesto definitely needed ther rest, but don't get it twisted they could've got that rest on the outside! Nesto finally caught up with Finesse "how many days we been down?" Finesse asked with a smirk. "Shit, too long!" Nesto shot back with a little bit of humor capturing the attention of everybody in the room. It took them about 2 and half hours just to get to the bus and about a half hour to get to the courthouse. Nesto took the time to catch up on everything going on in each of their units. "Ay Nesse, so you know Lollipop sent me a kite through my mamma telling me to hit her when I get out . . . . What you think?" Nesto asked. "Is that right" Finesse asked "you know that bitch is stupid trouble, I don't even know why you getting started wit her" Finesse said in protest. "That's for me to know and for you to find out nigga!!" Nesto rebuttled as he laughed hysterically. They were waiting to get called in to their attorney visit and to see the judge. The co put them in a room with a T.V that didn't work. The room was so philthy that it looked like ninja turtles lived there. "La prince! . . . . Pierr! . . . . Attorney visit!!" The C.O yelled.

Door swung open and some george jefferson tea-bag head looking nigga slid up in there talking some slick shit. The threads he wore looked like something worn by an american gangster. "Wassup fellas?" Mcdagger said talking fastly. "I got some good news and some bad news, what do you want to hear first?" Mcdagger said with a serious look on his face. Shit, now he had them thinking . . . . "The good news!" Finesse blurted out anxiously. "The good news is that I got your bail dropped down from 80,000 to 30,000" mcdagger said "so muthafucka whats the bad news?" Finesse said rowdily. "The bad news is that I cant get you out today because you have too many charges and the prosecution wants to hold you guys another two weeks" mcdagger stated non-cholantly and did it moving out the door. "Call me!" He said as he pranced off like he had a stick stuck in his ass. Man they had put the money they saved, up front to this guy and he couldn't even shake some burglary charges. "It's over for him" Finesse said. Nesto didn't worry about it. Another two weeks, that was cruise control. He did understand where Finesse was coming from though, you don't know the feeling of rejection when you think your going home. They made it to the end of the line and went through two doors when a clean cut C.O said "la prince and Pierr!" You made bail. They looked at each other and smiled, the game god was good and christmas came early. Finesse and Nesto were definitely ready for thir return. "You boys have any property you want to recover from the santa rita facility?" The C.O. Said . . . . "Nuthin!!" They both yelled out in harmony not wanting to look one more time at that filthy place that had held chains around their next for the past couple of months. After they changed out and walked through two metal detectors . . . . They got to the last door and both of their mouths dropped when they seen who bailed them out.

CHP 3
A FAMILIAR FACE

When they seen who bailed them out, their mouths dropped to the floor. The caramel mocha frappucino skinned 5ft 7 jazzy, supermodel, looking diva stood looking at them from behind her chanel shades while reapplying her pink shimmery lip gloss. She was carrying two big gucci bags that complimented the Dolci & Gabana skirt suit that look like it had been painted on her lusious body. Nesto knew a lot of women that acted like they were training for the olympics to get that weight off, but this girl was blessed in all the right places. It was Lollipop, now they didn't know that what she was there for but they were all ears. "Hey Daddy" she said as her red bottom stilletos jackhammered the floor trying to get to Nesto. "Move out my way nigga!!" She said with a smirk, as she slipped pass Finesse. "Damn . . . You know this might sound crazy, but im actually feelin your style" Finesse said with a wide grin. "Nigga . . . Don't try to jump on board now, cuz if you wasn't my Daddy's right hand man . . . . Uggh . . . I woulda been turned left on your ass, . . . Trust!" She said, as she gave Finesse a cold look. "Anywayz baby, I went to court today too, and they didn't want to let a bitch out, so I had to reach in my bra on em!!" Lollipop said as she arrogantly demonstated by touching her breasts inside of her shirt. "So I decided to get my baby out too so we can get some of this money together". She said with a wink. She then pulled some keys out of her purse and held them over her head to disable the car alarm on her 500 sl mercedez benz that Nesto knew would be a good look for him. "Here, this is for you Daddy" she proclaimed, as she handed both of the gucci bags to them and made it around the car to gain entry into her high price piece of black on black eye-candy. "Ay Nesto fareal, you be a lucky ass lil nigga sometimes, I don't know what they see in yo little black ass" Finesse said hatin', then climbed in the back. Man when they got in her car it was fully decked out you hear me?? Black leather interior, maybach seats, 20" flat-screen hangin from the roof, right in the middle of the two front sun-visors. The tinted windows were so black that you couldn't see anything inside. Pioneer deck with a 8" screen. She put the mini-zap board on her lap and used the remote to turn the volume up. She had gucci mane and O.J the juiceman going full force on the trunk. "Quarter-brick, half-a-brick, whole brick eegghhy!". When they finally got to open their bags, there were brand new akoo outfits, the new limited edition Jordan retro's, and all the accessories to go with them, socks, boxers, and t-shirts still in the pack. She even had them a tooth-brush and tooth paste travelers kit. She was definitely on top of her game. "Thank you baby, Nesto said with much appreciation and reached across the center council and gave her one of those mafia pecks on the cheek. When Nesto looked back, Finesse had the exact same things just in different colors. "So while I was down I had my lil young bitch holdin shit down for me" Lollipop said peeping in her rearview. "So what that shit got to do wit us?" Nesse snapped at her like a firecracker as if she was about to say some shady shit. "Nuthin to do with you . . . nigga", im talkn to Nesto so mind your fuckin' business" Lollipop said with authority. "N-e-wayz like I was sayn before I was rudely interrupted, I got some solid ass bitches runnin this paper game for me right now; checks, passports, travelers checks, sliders and all the shit. Lollipop said. "So how authentic we looking?" Nesto asked. "All my shit is authentic Nesto, you know I wouldn't even waste your time. I got the best paperwork movin rite now, and my home-girl is a teller at the bank up there on lakeshore." Lollipop boasted. Nesto thought, this may have been the break they've been waiting on. "It's good . . . Whatever",Nesto assured her because that's how they really felt. They were fresh out the box, barely on four wheels and needed to do something with themselves fast. As soon as they got back to Oakland, they hit a couple of corners off of 98th, smoked a couple of sticks and ended up somewhere in the hills off golf-links. When they pulled up they wondered what business she had at a mansion such as this one. Both Nesto and ness got out of the car and followed her in the house. "Welcome to my home fellas" she said in a sexy voice while directing them to remove their shoes. "Mi casa es su casa, at least until you piss me off!!" She laughed. When they got throught the door, she had a chandlier the size of a space ship hangin low enough to beam up some earthlings. The crystals glistened off of it as though it was covered with diamonds. They walked through the living room it was perfectly decorated with black art, pictures of malcolm x, martin luther king, hewey newton, and barak obama. She definitely had taste. It had to be at least a 62" plasma flat-screen that was hanging from the ceiling. She had snow white furniture with red accent pillows and snow white plush carpet to match, a bar in the corner with every drink that you could possibly think of, and pictures of her with stars that had been in there, on her wall. "This is my living room" she modeled and took them into the kitchen . . . Damn . . . Even the walls were coke white, Finesse thought as he looked around. There were marble countertops, and a big body chrome refridgerator, freezer and stove. She had every kind of fruit you could name on the table, from oranges to pineapples. After they left the kitchen, she took them through a hallway, and pulled on a book that was tilted on a bookshelf. The bookshelf turned sideways and made two paths available behind the bookshelf's wall. They followed her inside then down some stairs. The blare of loud music got louder & louder. When they finally got to the bottom and opened the door, they had never seen so many beautiful black women together having such a good time without any men involved. They felt like they were really in heaven. "This is the black hole fellas! Lollipop said winking. "What happens in the hole . . . Stays in the hole.". Nesse looked around and realized that he was definitely in paradise. He went to have a seat at the bar not able to take his eyes off of all the lusious women. Lollipop ordered a lemon drop, and Nesto ordered a rum and coke. Finesse then ordered a shot of patron. They were finally home, and needed every bit of this kick-back time. They got all caught up while Lollipop filled them in on where she was at with the whole get money thing. She wanted them to watch her back, with the moves she was making. It was something definitely to discuss. This was real round-table business. Finesse had everything he needed; drank, hoes, weed, and cash on the way. Nesto held him a spot in the corner and got in where he fit in. Nesto left Finesse in the lounge with all the exotic ladies and escaped to the master bedroom with Lollipop. Now for real, he thought, this could be no more than some head, some ass, and no feelings. It could be no other way, because they were too much alike. When they got to the bedroom Lollipop immediately made her way to the bathroom to make her some bath water. She dimmed the lights, burned a candle, and slipped out of all her clothes. Nesto had been taking county showers for the last couple of months so he didn't mind joining in. They both stripped down to their skin. The naked possessions of his penis hung swell all the way to the shower. She loved every minute of it. He washed her up and she washed him down, they rubbed skin to the point that she felt his manhood and couldn't wait to feel it inside of her. You could say they both enjoyed every minute of it. Lollipops whole body was stupid bangin. Her breast sat up on her chest so perfect. They were the size of cantelopes and her nipples were as round as silver dollars. Her ass was so round and plump that it looked like she had two basketballs stuck to it. From the looks of her cookie box, she took the initiative to keep that thang nice and neat. This was the type of fly shit that Nesto had always been into. This was definitely the life. It was pitch black in the bathroom, except the glare from the candles. She sat down in the water. He sat down right behind her and put his dick on her back. Nesto slid his hands down the rounds of her breast, then he layed back and let the moment grab a hold of him. They finished up with their bath made their way to the bed. When they reached it, she gently pushed him down, wrapped her lips around the tip of his dick and began with slow strokes, paying close attention to his reaction made her really get into it. She did her best to satisfy him. He reached down and placed his fingers in her honey spot, two inside her drooling pussy and one on her clitoris as he then lowered his face to place his toungue on it . . . Lollipop screamed in ecstasy as she held on to his head to keep him in the right spot. Nesto realized that if he was going to get in her purse, he would have to kill it, she was going to need a sample of the near death experience. He was about to knock her screws loose. When he finally slid his dick inside . . . . "Aaaawwwwww sssssshhhiiitt!! She yelled out in pleasure, she had felt the pipe, and he was straight, straight to the lane with a whole lot of power. It was nights like this that he really missed. Nesto guaranteed you wouldnt catch a glimpse of anything close to what he had right there layed up with him, inside those grimey santa-rita walls. When you did, it was the female deputys, or in a dirty magazine hidden under an inmates mattress. Nesto and Lollipop had layed up for a while before she actually dozed off. After a couple of hours of fucking, Lollipop was dead to the world. She slept hard with her mouth wide open. Those lips just did't look the same without being around his dick, he thought in his head and just sat back and laughed. He put his clothes back on and slipped downstairs to join the party. As he sat at the bar and had a couple of drinks . . .

He thought of how she told him how much she enjoyed his company and would like to continue to use his services. She told him about an inside job she had for him to get him back on his feet. She told him about Moco. Moco was her little girlfriend that she had workin in the bank. She explained everything he needed to hear. When he finally decided to get up from the bar, he seen Finesse holding up a table in the center of the room. "Call me" by too short & lil kim, was bumpin in the speaker boxes hangin from each corner of the room. There was two really pretty girls on the top of the table where Finesse was sitting. They shook the lint off their asses right in Finesse's face. He had his own bottle of patron now, and looked like he was really being entertained. All the other women were in their own ecstacy and hypnotized by the music that had their bare nakedness gyrating. Nesto knew that this one night could not take them off track, although they needed it. They were fresh out and eager to shine. Lollipop told Nesto that she wanted him to call a meeting tomorrow. They all needed to sit down at the roundtable, and figure out exactly how and when the next move would go down. Nesto and Finesse would need all their sleep. After Nesto had a couple of more drinks with Nesse, he slid back to bedroom and went straight to sleep. Tomorrow would be a long day.

CHP 4
ROUND TABLE BUSINESS

When they awoke the next morning, Lollipop was in the shower, so Nesto slid downstairs to see what Nesse was up to. "Top of the morning bruh" Nesto announced as he made his way to the couch Nesto had slept on. If you didn't know him you would have swore that he was the prince of zimunda. He had not one! But two beautifully naked women comforting him. It reminded Nesto of the scene on coming to america when she says. "The royal penis is clean your highness." "Do I gotta get up?" Finesse complained when he realized how good he had it. "Yea bruh go head and get dressed and meet me on the balcony in 15!" Nesto said wit a little bit of militance. He rushed back upstairs and by that time, Lollipop was just stepping out the shower. The water jogged through trails all the way down her legs. "Damn this girl was bad" Nesto thought to himself. She lotioned her body up and down then flaunted her fingers across the lips of her vagina and moaned as she groaped herself. "I know what you need" she said casually as she strolled over to the armior that was in the corner of the room. She opened it and pulled out about a half ounce of weed. "Now you going into my stash!" She declared with a smile. If she didn't just read his mind. He thought. She handed him a box of 60 cigarillos. "Im bout to roll up, so meet me on the balcony" Nesto said as he left the room. Before Nesto got back to the balcony, he stopped in the kitchen. Nesto found a jar of coffee and a pot. He put on a pot of hot water. When he finally got to the balcony, he passed Finesse the swisher and weed to roll up. Nesto enjoyed early morning smoke sessions, it was literally how he loved to start his day. "So what you do last night?" Nesse asked eager to get some info "everythang!!" Nesto said thinking about the grammy he won. "Come on . . . . Keep it a hunnid!" Nesse said smiling. "Ok, it was straight . . . Shit he aint complaining" Nesto said laughing and pointed to his dick. "Well I had two bitches . . . One on my waist, and one on my face" Finesse said crazily. "Shit . . . Can I get a refill!" He added "bruh you crazy as hell" Nesto said "I kno, im a freak like dat!" Nesse confessed and started laughing. Nesto and Nesse got intoxicated with laughter while Nesto grabbed and gutted the two swishers and filled them with the weed they were about to smoke. "I definitely could get use to this" Nesse said. "Nah ness, this just our stepping stone" Nesto told Nesse as he finished rolling the blunts. Lollipop stepped out of the sliding glass door looking like americas next top model. She had on some red stilettos, a tight see through white sun dress that would have held up traffic on the hoe stroll. She had a red bra and matching thong on underneath with her long black beautiful hair hangin halfway down her back. "Just in time baby" Nesto said "I know" Lollipop shot back "im always on time" she added as she sat down on his lap. Nesto lit the blunt and hit it a couple of times. You could taste the grapes. The weed was so good, that Nesto gave her a peck on da cheek as he damn near coughed up a lung. "Aight, so fellas we got a couple of moves to make today." Lollipop started "then a little bit of shopping tomorrow yall wit it?" She asked "first things first" she said. "I need to run to my homegirl's house in berkeley to get this paperwork, and then I'll be back to get you guys alright? "Yall should be all shit, showered, and shaved by the time I get back" Lollipop said, as she made her way to the door. "Dueces" she said and she was gone. If she had to run all the way to the b-town Finesse and Nesto had plenty of time to get ready. "The bitch seems a little sharper than the rest" Finesse said. "Yea, but let me worry about that" Nesto said "we got shit to do as men, so just enjoy the ride getting back to the money!" Nesto said. By the time they got done smoking, it looked like heaven. He went back upstairs to the bedroom to get in the shower. The full glass shower was nice. Looked like Nesto could pile 4 naked women next to him. After he took care of his hygiene thang he felt like a new man. "Shit all a nigga need is a haircut" he mumbled to himself looking in the mirror.

"You a pretty black muthafucka" he said to himself then continued to get dressed. About an hour passed before he was all the way ready. In the meantime, he did what any real nigga would do . . . . Scoped out the room and looked for anything to attract his attention. When he got to the dresser, the first drawer only had lingirie and thongs. The real thongs too, the ones that look like shoe strings. The second drawer was full of mail, letters and papers that looked like copies of rental reciepts. When he got to the third drawer it was locked! "Looking for something?" Lollipop said as he spun around caught red handed. "Yea where the fuck is the deodorant" Nesto shot back. Lollipop strolled to the hallway closet and tossed Nesto the deodorant. "You guys ready? We got a lot to do today" she said. Shortly after they grabbed everthing they needed, they headed downstairs to get ness and cut. When they got downstairs, Nesto noticed Finesse harassing a new face. She was tall and petite, and her facial features could have been compared to taraji p. Henson or somebody, she was kool!. "This my girl yall! . . . Me and this bitch go back like ripper slippers" Lollipop said laughing "aww hell naw, not ripper slippers!" Finesse died laughing. "She gone rock with us today and help us get this money together" Lollipop said. That was one thing Nesto loved about that girl. She always had a purse full of tricks. "Yall niggas need to get it together, yall looking trife" Moco said jokingly. "We gon take care of yall though!" Moco added with insurance. "Man fuck trife, you niggas looking endangered. Aint too many niggas left looking like yall" Lollipop carried on with the shananigans. "Aight so look!" She started "ness, you going with Moco and Nesto of course you riding with me." She added. "And when we done we meet back in the middle." Moco said adding her two cent. You could just tell that they had this shit down to a science. Gotta love solid women that know what they're doing. Lollipop pulled out a big manilla envelope and divided the paperwork. She took half and gave half to Moco. When Nesto and ness stepped outside they knew the lime life was coming. Moco had a hot pink 745 with hot pink dipped rims, matching race car seats, and pitch black tint. Moco and Lollipop were definitely having it their way and ness and Nesto just needed one good lick to put them back on their feet. Nesto had a good feeling that today would be that day. "Smootches!" Moco yelled as they went their separate ways. "Take care of my brody" Nesto shouted at Moco. Grabbing the handle to lollipops car . . . "Oh . . . He good!" Moco said sassily and that was it, they were gone. Lollipop lit a newport, then stretched back in her seat as if she was in deep thought. "So we gone tear up everything on the other side of the caldecott tunnel, and they gon run through frisco" Lollipop said filling Nesto in on the planned events. "We got twenty banks to hit . . . . And they got twenty" Lollipop continued as cool as a cube of ice. "After we make these moves baby, we can start on our future, we can buy a new house in puerto rico, and . . . ." And before Lollipop could finish going off on a tangent, Nesto stopped her dead in her tracks. "Slow down ma, let's stay focused on this revenue and take it one day at time. I just wanna see you doing better . . . With me baby" Lollipop added sadly. "I know baby . . . I respect it" Nesto said keeping it short and simple. Lollipop reached in her purse as they pulled up to a stop light. She passed Nesto a hand full of payroll checks with different business names on them. "Are all the routing numbers and shit legit?" Nesto asked as he scanned through them. "Shit . . . . Too legit to quit!" She saidsmiling and pretending to do the mc hammer dance in her seat. They entered interstate 580 freeway then cut through the warren freeway all the way around by walnut creek under the caldecott tunnel. When Nesto scanned the checks, none of the checks were more or less than 900 dollars. Lollipop said they could "ride around getting it" all day without those having to be verified. They made their rounds to every bank they could find that was on the way to walnut creek. When she entered the first bank, it was made clear just how easy it was. "Wait here" lolliipop saidas she went in to see how long the line was. She returned back to the car two minutes later and said that she would be back in 15 minutes. Nesto watched the clock on the stereo in the car. It was 12:45 when she went in and 12:59 when she came out. "Like butta baby" she said as nine crispy hundred dollar bills fell from her hands and dropped into Nesto's lap. "That easy huh?" Nesto asked with an impressed smile. "That easy baby!" Lollipop shot back smiliing happy that she could be of some assistance to a real nigga. They did the same routine for about 4 and a half hours. Nesto called Moco to check on ness. They told him that they were just bout wrapping it up soon. The conversation didn't last long, more like a check in. By the time Lollipop and Nesto got to their last bank Nesto was scared as hell holding all that fast money. He knew right then and there that any small slips would have the feds all up in the mix. "Today was kool tho!" Nesto thought in his mind. Everthing went as planned on their end. By the time they got back to lollipops house they had 18 Stacks(18 thousand dollars) that they made in less than eight hours. Shit, when you was getting money like this who the fuck wanted to work right?. Thirty minutes later they heard Moco's 745 pulling up inside the gate. Nesto and Lollipop was tickled by all the giggling they did, like they had known each other for years. You know they say time flies when your havin fun. Making money was always fun for Nesto. "Honey im home" Moco said as she came in the house joking. "Ness had two fanz!" Talking bout fanning hella money. After he was done demonstrating how his day turned out it was time to count the scratch. Nesto could feel the slob dripping from his lips like a hungry pitt bull needing to be fed. They headed into the dining room and everybody pulled up a chair. Boy did they have fun counting that money. Nesse kept reinacting that part from belly "count da money! . . . Count dat fuckin money" Lollipop had those fancy money machines so it made runnning through a lot of money much faster. When the last dolla hit the table, they had racked up a good 36 Stacks. Nesto went to work in his head trying to figure out the math. That was 9 Stacks a piece. Nesto had seen Stacks here and there but never that much at one time. It didn't stop there either. After a few more runs with Lollipop and Moco, by the end of the week they had 180 Stacks but by the end of the month they had accumulated a little bit more than 720 thousand cold cash. Shit it had been thirty days today that ness and Nesto had been home, so it was time to sit it down and figure out their next move. They had the dough now, so the only question at hand was . . . What the hell were they going to do with it?.

CHP 5

Nesto and ness woke up the next morning with a new attitude about themselves. Shit a month ago, they were fresh out the can and didn't have shit but a helping hand. As you can see you catch on to the right one it may take you a long way. After they ran the paperwork with Lollipop they both had almost twenty g's a piece to play with. Today Lollipop had plans to run them down to some car auction in benecia so they could flip some wheels. "Wassup baby?" Lollipop said as she slid downstairs to where Nesto and ness was. "Nuthin much" Nesto replied as he gave her a seductive look that complimented her short skirt. Nesto and Nesse had gotten so use to the balcony, because they loved the view of the bay area. At night all you seen was a million bright lights shining over the city. When they finished the morning session up, Nesto looked at ness and swore he looked like a black china man the way the weed pulled his eyes to a squint. Both of their eyes was tight, they had smoked at least a eigth of some grandaddy. That was some of the best weed you could find, Oakland california had it honest. When the last blunt layed to rest, Nesto looked at the dubee filled ashtray "man if those were real roaches you'd be in trouble Lollipop" Nesto said jokingly to fill the silence that had took over. "Fa sho . . . . But huh . . . Don't even jinx me like that!" She said joking back. It took about forty-five minutes for them to make it out there to benecia. When they got out there, it was a differnt type of auction from the one they usually had. The first thing they saw was boats and harleys. As they moved more to the center of the lot they seen all the things that got seized by police during major drug busts and raids, and were now back on the market. They even had nice foreclosed houses in a catalogue for them to see. Nesto felt like a kid in a Candy store browsing all the toys they had to play with. Him and Nesse must have looked over cars for about an hour before they actually seen something they liked for a reasonable price. Even though they had "money to blow" they were not trying to spend more than four g's a piece. "Bruh check this one out" Finesse said in a frenzy. When Nesto turned around it was a black lexus coupe 430 fully loaded. "Yea . . . Thats you bruh" Nesto said. "That black on black would definitely be a good look for me too" Finesse said as he "pictured himself rollin'." "Hey and that's you right there Nesto!" Lollipop said as she pointed to the car right next to it. "Yall could be twinz" she said smiling. It was the same exact car that Nesto had just pointed out to ness. "Nah, that aint my swag!" Nesto said as he kept browsing. Nesto was already doing numbers in his head. He knew they would need different whips so they could switch them up. Because that's what niggas had to do when shit got hot. After he turned a couple more aisles, Nesto fell in love when he seen a burnt orange camaro ss already on rims and kitted out. They had each spent about thirty-two hundred dollars by the time it was all over with. That was the perks about riding out to the auction . . . A majority of the time, you left with what you came for. After nobody else bidded on the cars they had their eyes on, they made the proper arrangements to come back and pick them up the next day with cash in hand. Nesto's city had a lot of rubber on the ground from niggas showin out and bringin they car to the sideshows . . . Nesto and the gmb click would hybernate all winter fixing they shit up just to go dumb in the summer. Them niggas really had a thing for cars. They definitely didn't mind taking on a good project. Before wild ass shit start happening at the sideshows, there wasn't a weekend that you couldn't catch Nesto and Finesse there showin out. They loved to bring their trophies out. But now, cars filled with hyphy ass youngstas took over the streets . . . It was like a whole nother world going on at these hours of the night . . . And everybody was woke . . . Wide awake at like 4 am like it was 4 pm. Different cars zig-zagged back and forth down the boulevards with all the doors open and their sound systems on blast. Nesto and Nesse were definitely part of the reason shit like that stayed moving through the bay. This was the life they struggled to get away from. They were usually there in the streets when it went down after 2am. Every weekend when Nesto and the gmb click got out of the clubs and had indulged in their last drink, they usually saw their friends passing them by in the traffic riding recklessly up and down the blocke tr. This shit had been going on for years, every since Nesto and Nesse's daddies were in the game. Nesto just smiled, looked up and thanked god when he thought about what they had been through and what he had done for them. When ness and Nesto rode around extra clean they had to keep their eyes open for them suckaz, because they knew that they might just try to rob them cuz them niggas had that glow. "Im getting cake like erry day my birthday" j stalin an up and coming artist from west Oakland jammed recklessly in the speakers, as they rode back to the town. They must've blazed about four more sticks and took a detour to check a couple of traps before they actually passed back through Oakland. Nesse said he wanted to hit southland mall so he could pick up some more gear before they went back to lollipops. About ten or fifteen minutes later they were exiting interstate 880 on Winton St, headed for the mall which was right off of the exit and not that far at all. "Nesto you gotta see these new akoo jeans, they bussin bruh" Nesse said all excited. "They da cleanest lil jeans I done seen so far as of some new shit" he added. It felt good to them to have money and do whatever they wanted to. This what life was all about to them, bossing up and keeping god first! They picked up a few things, Nesto got chain for his neck that hung to his dick. The ice in the cross had to be about 4 1/2 carats and he got away with it for about twelve-hundred dollars. Ness got on it too, you know they had to do their stunna man shit. That was mando! Nesto already had a fat timepiece that his moms had bought him for his twenty-first birthday. She was the one that put him on to highline jewelery in the first place. They were the next best thing to tom's and spitz and those were just a few to name of the hood jewelers. Highline had definitely seen a fare share of his money and they saw nuthin but dollar signs everytime they seen him. They hit shiekhs and picked up a couple of pair of shoes, then went to macy's to get a couple of fits, after that . . . They both agreed that they had spent enough money for the day. "You niggas hollywood now huh, acting all brand new . . . . Look at you!" Lollipop said as she decided to showcase some humor. She grabbed Nesto's arm and was just happy to be in the presence of someone solid. On their way out Lollipop grabbed her a couple of things while Nesto and ness flirted with the little hootchies walking past "eeerrrfff!" Ness barked at one. Man he was silly as hell. When Lollipop was satisfied with what she had, she paid cash and threw it in the bag. "I see yall looking good now Daddy! Don't it feel good?" She asked sounding like a motivational speaker. It was something about her that made Nesto enjoy having her around. When he thought about it "she had really put them back in the game. They owed her big time, just to show some appreciation for everything, Nesto bought her some canary diamond studs, and had them wrapped in a pretty little velvet box. When they got back to the house it was packed as usual the girls might as well had signed the lease because they never went home. When they opened the door it was like a party that never ended. Finesse got dragged off by some haitian meagan goode looking little bitch. As Nesse slid off he said "her lip gloss is poppin" and started dancing. That brotha was crazy as hell sometimes but he definitely knew how to enjoy himself. They both just laughed from the stupid comment. Nesto took Lollipop upstairs and they stuck to the script. "You know I really appreciate everything you been doing for me" he told her "and tonight we gon do things a little different" Nesto said. "Is that right Daddy?" "What you gone do to me Mr. Man" she asked comically, ready to do a little roll playing. "That's for me to know and you to find out" he told her with his controlling voice. Nesto thought about how women liked it when you talk to them like that and smiled to himself. Nesto thought hard about how to execute his plan especially for a woman who was so use to being in charge. He went in the bathroom, lit the candles and turned on the shower. The steam filled the room so quickly that it felt like a sauna. Lollipop suggested Nesto get started in the shower as she went back downstairs to get the 'moscato bubbly' she had chilling in the fridge. He complied and was all lathered up by the time she undressed and slid in with him. He instantly grabbed her olay body wash put some soap on her shower pouf then gently rubbed the lips of her vagina, but went no further. He washed her entire body up good, and she did him back. She always said that their physical attraction was dangerous because she felt like her pussy was platinum enough to tie him down. He didn't think so, he was playin just to play. He left her in the shower and made his way to the room. He lit the candles that were in the four corners if the room. He grabbed the remote and turned the radio station to "the quiet storm" 102.9 KBLX. Radio station and fired up some dro while he waited for her to get out. He placed the earrings on the nightstand so she could see them when she got out, the mood was set and Nesto had planned to make this one of the best nights she ever had. She exited the shower without a towel and her wet body made him want her even more. He began stroking himself as she lotioned up and draped herself with oils from bath and body works, Lollipop grabbed her perfume and sprayed her neck, then her wrist, and rubbed them together. "Cool water baby!" What you know about that?" She said seductively. The truth is, it should have been called "climaxx" because the smell, along with her sexy naked black ass made nestos dick stand straight up. As she set the perfume bottle on the nightstand, she noticed the earrings as her eyes lit up . . . "Thank you sooo much Daddy", she whispered in nestos ear as she slid right on top of him, pushed him down and started to gyrate her pussy as fast as she could. Her nipples were so perfect that they turned into stop signs as she held them up with her hands so he could suck them. He must have sucked and licked them alone for about fifteen minutes. Then he let his tongue escape down her body, passing her stomach until he got where she needed him to be. When his lips reached her pearl, she let out a moan to let him know he was in the right spot. The sounds that came from her mouth made it seem she was speaking to the gods in a foreign language. He slid his tongue up and down against her pearl a few more times. She purred . . . "Oooogggghhh!!! Aaaggghhh!!! Daddy, please don't stop" as he put his finger inside her to caress her g-spot. Lollipop felt like his dick and his tongue game was so tight, she would walk around with them in her purse if she could. Shit, it had been about 20 minutes since she got out the shower, and the foreplay was still crazy good as R. Kelly's "seems like your ready" softly played in the background. "Daddy wait" she whimpered right before she reached her peak, "I have a surprise for you too!" She got up and opened the closet door as Moco's sexy carmel colored naked ass pranced over to the bed where Nesto was laying and gently placed his dick in her mouth, she had been in there watching the whole scene and was ready! His eyes widened as Lollipop smiled with amazement. "Lets have fun Daddy" Lollipop said, as all three of them began the road to ecstacy.

CHP 6
BACK TO THE BASICS

When the sun came peeking in through the window, they layed motionless in bed, totally exausted from the pasts nights escapade. Nesto heard finesses footsteps down the hall as he yelled, "ay Nesto, yall come eat man!" They all could smell the scent of breakfast being prepared. "Goodmorning baby!!" Lollipop said, stroking his hard on. "Yea goodmorning Daddy" as Moco put her hand on top of lollipops, putting her 2 cents in, not wanting to feel left out. Nesto felt like the cat whisperer the way he put those 2 pussy's to sleep! Not wanting to get up he reached around and squeezed both of their asses pulling them closer as he chimed "damn, we gota do this shit more often". Moco gave Lollipop a smirkish grin, as if Lollipop had been holding nestos dick hostage. After a quick shower, they all headed downstairs to eat before the food got cold. When they got to the kitchen the breakfast was neatly prepared, from the spoons and forks to the plates and paper towels. Finesse has cooked, turkey sausage, grits, eggs, biscuits and topped it off with some sunny delight and fresh coffee. Nesto hadnt had a home cooked meal like that since he had ate at this soul food spot called "just like gramma's cookin". Nesto grabbed the remote and flipped television to the channel 2 news. It was new years day and the city was shook up of the shooting of oscar grant at the fruitvale bart station. It was said that him and his friends were at a party in frisco and had just got back to Oakland when the officer, johannes meserle shot the unarmed innocent blackman in cold blood, talking about he thought he pulled his tazer instead. The way he got off, you would have swore he was the head of the illuminati. People was protesting all over Oakland, tearing up shit and everything. Nesto jumped up all excited and decided he wanted in on the action. "Finesse come look at this shit bruh" as he pointed to the tv. After Nesse seen what was up, it was only a matter of minutes before they jumped in lollipops car and were on interstate 580 headed to downtown. In the midst of the riots, they decided to make footlocker their victim and stepped their shoe game up. Gotta love free shit from the riots right. It was on. After they got what they wanted, they jumped back on 580, called the girls and said meet them by the amc theater in emeryville, then headed to benecia to pick up their whips.

When Lollipop and Moco arrived, they had the appearances of some real barbie dolls, damn, these bitches were bad. They were truly best friends, they were not only the same size and shape, they even dressed alike. They came wearing form fitting louis vitton jackets over lace camisoles, black skinny jeans, black stilettos and louis vitton handbags to match.

Nesto fell asleep on the way there and the little nap did him some good, he woke up feeling rejuvinated. By the time he woke up they were already there, the girls let them out in the front and said they would meet up with later. "Call me if you need me ok" Lollipop screamed through the sunroof as they pulled off. As soon as they stepped foot in the sunlight, the bling from Nesse's new chain damn near blinded him. "That muthafucka is zappin" Nesto told him, "yea yo shit hittin too" Finesse added. He had on the outfit that he picked up from southland yesterday. He finally got the akoo jeans and the matching shirt with a million crazy designs on it, that he had been talking about so much. When they finally made it to the office where their paperwork for the cars was to be done, they met up with the same guy named frank from the day before, now frank looked like a retired mobster that started selling cars as a cover up. Nestos pops had always told him that you can always tell a good suit by the slits in the back of the coat and the creases that never fell out of the pants. Frank had on one of those. "How you fellas doin today?" He said in a raspy godfather like voice. He sounded like his nose was all congested like he had just snorted up peru. "Here are the extra keys and I will have my men bring your cars around shortly" frank said. "By the way, I left my card, along with allyour papers in the glove boxes, in case yall become interested in some property or what have you. You gentlemen have a nice day". After waiting another five minutes, they seen Finesse's lexus coupe, then Nesto's camaro ss. When they got a clear visual of the cars heading towards them, they couldn't help but notice there were two youngsters behind the wheels that looked like they really enjoyed their jobs. They heard the kid chirpin Nesto's ss as he switched gears getting to him. He couldn't wait to get behind that thang. After they threw a few dollars at the drivers, the wait was finally over and they were out! Boy did him and Nesse show their asses on the way back to the town.

Nesto was in 3rd gear all ready doing 100 miles per hour, Nesto seen Finesse's black on black thang in hot pursuit, coming up in the rearview. They criss crossed and did illegal lane changes all the way back. They were definitely back to the basics. Nesto slowed down to let Nesse catch up. With no music on, he heard the motor running like a champ. "Meet me at denny's in emeryville, Nesto said as he smoothly passed him. "Zoom!" They were at it again, showing their ass. When Nesto got to denny's, he found somewhere to park, then Nesse slid in right beside him. When the engines died down, they gave eachother that look that said "yea nigga we back". When they bounced out the car and went inside, they were greeted by a waitress that joyfully asked "table for 2?" "Please!" Nesse quickly said with a flirty gaze as he looked her up and down. She caught on fast as she licked her glossy lips and said "Do I know you?", "Do you want to get to know me is the real question" Nesse rebuttled . . . "Uhh huh maybe, if you give me a good enough reason" she replied now trying to act kinda shy. "Oh for sure, in due time hopefully" Nesse shot back. "Whats your name sis?" Nesto said just being nosey and trying to break the manotny." My name is patrice but friends and fam call me "platinum". "Now u bruthas figure out what you want to eat", she said as she seated them and slid them two menus, "and I will find somebody to take your order". She turned and walked back to her post to greet and seat customers as they came in, switching so hard that she made her panties creep up the crack of her ass. "Ay u know Nesto, I been seriously thinking about catching up with some of our old connects, and getting shit fired up one more time" Finesse suggested. "I mean we got money but. What we gone do, spend the shit til its gone, or do this shit the way we know how?". The look Finesse gave Nesto, spoke a thousand words. He was hungry, he was thirsty, and Nesto seen it all in his face. "To tell you the truth, ive been thinking about the same thing, but I want to work smarter not harder" "We gotta get a squad together, a machine together and just stay in the back field for now" Nesto said. "We aint got no time to be doin no more prison bids or county time. Feel me?" He told Nesse with the most serious face he could arrange. "True dat!" Finesse said, agreeing totally with what Nesto said. "You guys ready to order yet?" The little sexy waitress said as she came back stalking them. "Na lil ma we need a few more minutes" Nesto said as he browsed the menu like he didn't know what he wanted . . . The same thing he always ordered, an all american omelette with everything on it, no pork. Finesse wanted to make his own grand slam, so he ordered accordingly. They placed their orders as soon as she came back and told her that they would like to have milkshakes with it. "I get off at eight o'clock" she said as she slid ness a napkin with her cell number and facebook info on it. "What we need to do . . . Is get us some phones b!!" Nesto said joking with ness in his new york accent. "Word" Finesse said giving him a dose of his own medicine. "Like asap son! . . . Especially . . . If you plan on using that number" the waitress added excercising her sense of humor. "You know what? . . ." "I like you already!" Nesse laughed, after he picked up on what she said. "That's a good thing" she said as she put a twist in her switch and walked away. She stopped in mid stride, looked back, then looked down at her ass and back at Nesse, then kept it pushin. "She wants me!" Nesse said as he got caught up in a lustful daydream. "Fuck all that, you still got nitty number?" Nesto asked Finesse with a dazed face. "You know I do!" Finesse said sarcastically. "Well, I need you to call that nigga and get the prices together, while you doin that . . . imma talk to my folks about the "boats" Nesto said, which was basically a brick of ecstacy pills. Now nitty was a O.G nigga that Nesse knew. He came from new orleans after hurricaine katrina, and had made a name for himself around the town movin that work. He pick and chose who he wanted to deal with because he was a scary nigga fareal. He had so much work that sometimes he was scared to move it. Nesto knew he could get a boat of pills for no more than a grand a piece. The price of the pills now . . . . Verses when then first came out. The value decreased horribly because everybody in the city had them. It was always a hassle investing Nesto's money into them, because they just didn't move like they used to. That white girl, slang for cocaine, on the other hand, would keep the fiends running to the trap all night. Nesto had an asian connect out of this world on the weed. It was a light strand of purple, not too potent so, it was strictly come up weed. It wasn't the best, but it was far from the worst. The price was twenty-one hundred dollars a pound. You couldn't beat that wit a bat. Not to mention between hitting licks and growing they shit, they never ran out! Nesto and Finesse also had a buddy who ran bricks straight out the pharmacy and he would give them a total of ten 8oz bottlesof promethezine for five hundred dollars. This was crazy cuz ness and Nesto had took a trip to texas a couple summers ago and them niggas down there was really on that shit. They called it "lean". The one bottle they had taken with them, ended up selling for about five-hundred dollars. So basically they sold their one bottle for the price of what they would pay for ten of them, you do the math. After him and Nesse finished shooting the numbers around, they cut across the street to the powell street plaza, and picked up the new metro 4g smartphone. They thought about going sprint, t-mobile, verizon, or any of that shit because they had the money, but fuck all that . . . hood niggas like hood shit . . . Nesto said to himself and didn't want to let money change them. They figured they used the phone so much, that they were better off with that metro flat rate anyway. Don't that just sound like some shit a nigga would do? Nesse laughed to himself as he passed the cashier his money! "Hey what up Nesto" somebody said, trying to catch his attention as they exited the metro store. It was Stackz and he was fresh out. "When you get out the can?" Nesto asked? "Shit I just touched down a few days ago" Stackz said "ya need to put ya boy on" tryin to land his hands in something. "Yea, imma think about that" Nesto said stroking the hairs on his chin looking Stackz straight in his eyes trying to read him. "As a matter of fact I got a lil something up right now . . . but shit we just now getting situated our damn selves. Yah mean?" Nesse said ready to point some fingers and do some gorilla work. They all used their phones to exchange numbers, gave Stackz a fist pound and then hopped back in their whips. Ness had a 415 number, which was san francisco's area code. Niggas played with their numbers like that sometimes just to throw a motha fucka off. Nesto told ness that he had to care of a few things and that he would catch up with him later. The reality of the situation was that it was time to pay baby momma a visit. Nesto had two of them. One of them was so evil that he couldn't stand her mean ass but he had love for her regardless. Shit, he always said. "She might try to argue with president obama for saying the wrong thing to her ass". As for the other one, he never figured out why she liked to call the police so much. That ole police calling ass b@*%& seemed to have them on speed dial. He couldn't live with her, but couldn't live without her. She stayed in East Oakland somewhere in the dirty thirties. She stayed somewhere close to one of Nesto's old neighborhoods, off of brookdale ave. When he got to his baby momma's house he was not ready for all the shit he saw. He turned the key and opened the door to find his baby momma jumpin up and down on some niggas dick, while his sons were only in the next room watching nickelodeon. That pussy must have been good to him because that bitch ass nigga was moaning louder than she was. "Nesto . . . Damn . . . What the fuck?" She screamed with terror in her eyes as Nesto was stuck and didn't know what to do for the first few seconds. His babymomma jumped up and covered herself. "What the fuck you doin here nigga" this swiss beatz looking nigga yelled "and who the fuck are you anyway" he kept on . . . "Who the fuck am I??" Nesto repeated, looking around the room, until he spotted an empty heineken bottle sitting on the counter next to him. He picked it up and hit him with it. "Now get the fuck out" Nesto said as he tried to connect every last blow he could get in before the nigga got all the way out the door. He grabbed him by the face and told em "next time I catch you here, it aint gon be no glass bottle ima hit you with" Nesto said kicking him in the ass as he ran off.

"Bitch you really need to get your shit together!" He told her. "Fuck you Nesto! You don't wanna fuck with me, so how you just gone come up in here acting like you the man of my house and shit?" She cried "the same reason you up in here fucking niggas for free on the living room floor and the kids ain't even sleep yet . . . You lil trifilin ass bitch!" Nesto added full of anger. He was mad as hell. "Anywayz I came by here to drop you off some money so you can get my boys whatever they need and you in here fuckin the next nigga like your life depended on it" Nesto continued unable to look her in the eyes. He was already mad at her for fucking this one nigga he grew up with, while he was locked up, so you know he had to go hard on her. He reached in his pocket and peeled off twenty crispy hundred dollar bills and made it rain on her naked ass. "A bitch is a bitch, but a hoe makes money . . . . So which one are you?" He often showed her tough love, but he really worried about her sometimes . . . Nesto shook his head in disgust, then made his way to the kids door . . . "Jordan and fresh . . . Let's go!!" Nesto yelled for the kids. The kids came running and he took them exactly how they were!

CHP 7
REALITY CHECK

Nesto brought the boys with him so they could get some fresh air. When they spent time together he always tried to catch up on everything he missed. "So what's new son?" Nesto said to Jordan, his oldest boy who always had something to talk about. "Today we recited some of barack obamas inaugural speech in class, hey Daddy, don't you know he is the first black president?" We are learning so many new cool things in my school. Don't you wish you went to my school?" He said excitedly . . . Nesto smiled and shook his head in agreement. Nesto's other son fresh was just so happy to get out the house, that he jumped up and down grunting out words that were not yet known to the human language. For a one year old, he only knew a few words that would make you take a second look. His favorite word was "bitch" and even though he couldnt talk, he always said it at the right time. Please believe he was more of a charmer when he was happy. Nesto's oldest son had just made five, so they threw him a huge laser tag party at scandia in vacaville. It was quality time like that, that sometimes made him regret things not working out with their mother. Nesto also had a daughter, "harmony",that was his oldest child, she lived in richmond. It was her mother that he had the most problems with. They decided to name her "harmony" because that was the only time they actually got along. Nesto thought, it was just his daughters momma's anger of not understanding why things didn't work out with them. He was in the middle of a custody battle with her to try to get his daugher every other weekend. He could hear the anger in her voice everytime he thought about it. "Why you had to take me to court nigga? . . . you know you can see your daughter anytime you get ready!" She would sarcastically say . . . . Well that was just about true, when she wasn't actin funny. The bottom line was, within that same year, a few things changed when he was working and barely had time to spend with her like he wanted. When he didn't have a job and had plenty of time to spend with her, he had to muster up the strength to deal with her mother. She couldn't have him so she wanted to make his life a living hell. "Dad when is harmony, me, fresh and you going to be a family again?" Jordan asked curiously. Nesto took a deep breath and thought of the best truthful answer he could give him. "Well basically son, your dad has done alot of messing up in his life . . . . You understand?" Jordan nodded in agreement. "And the only way we all can be a family again is when your dad gets his life together and stops messin up out here, you understand that too?" He nodded once more and said "well you need to stop messing up fast dad!" Nesto just laughed, thinking. This kid was growing up too fast. The fact of the matter was that Nesto knew his son was absolutely right. Every major risk Nesto had ever took was to better his situation and to try to get him and his family by, even in his adolescent frame of mind. The grown man inside of him knew that a real man woke and up went to work everyday, then came home to spend time with his family instead of running the streets. Shit, god knew that Nesto wanted to do the family thing so bad, but it just never quite worked out like that. He wanted the big house, with the backyard somewhere decent where his kids could grow up, run around and play. A dog, a nice car and a good woman with a good head on her shoulders that would be there for him when he needed her, but that was all in due time. Nesto knew, nothing ever happened over night . . . nothing!. If he was about to get back in the game, he knew that he would have to get in and get out because death didn't wait for no man. With the murder rate at an all time high in the streets of Oakland, he knew anybody could get it. "I love you dad" Jordan announced "uuughhh! Da-da . . . . Luv-yuu!" Fresh grunted as he put his bid in as well. "I love yall too, and thats why yall gotta learn everything that you can for Daddy because your pops is gonna be an old man one day, and I will need yall to take care of me." He coached. "It will make your Daddy so happy to see you guys grow up, graduate from school and do more with your lives than I did" he said, meaning every word that came from his heart. "Im trying to stay grounded in you guys life, because I let down the people who had big hopes for me when I was growing up, you understand?" Nesto asked, actually tearing up a little, fresh nodded his head like he really understood too. Nesto seen so much of himself in those kids, so he knew he had only the right decisions left to make, but still had to do what he had to do for now. After Nesto spent some time with them, they left the mini park across the street from their house and went to micky "d's" at eastmont, for happymeals, he then took them back home before it started getting dark. Nesto gave Jordan his new number and told him to call him if he needed him. As soon as Nesto walked out, Nesse hit him on his mobile phone. "Wasup brah?" He answered "what you got movin?" He said "not too much just got done spending some time with da boyz, as he paused and smiled to himself . . . ." It made Nesto feel good to be able to say that because alot of niggas he knew, didn't give a damn about their kids or even be bothered with them at all. Well that wasn't him, and he was determined that if he couldn't be a husband to their mother, to at least to learn how to be a good father. Nesto was tired of not being able to live the glamorous life with his kids involved, so it was clearly time to make arrangements. "Ehy Nesto! You still there, snap out of it!" Nesse said as he came back in over the line sounding frustrated from the silence of nestos thoughts. "You good dog? . . . you need a hug?" He said playfully trying to cheer him up. "Nah . . . . Im good I just need to get shit together before it's too late you know? A nigga gettin too old for this street shit Nesse. Im bout to be thirty . . . In a couple of months and still don't have a pot to piss in or a window to throw it out of." Nesto complained. "And im tired of staying with these hoes who just throw me out when shit start goin bad . . ." "We need our own" they both said at the same time in full agreement of every word. Nesse knew that Nesto was speaking the truth . . . . Hopefully sooner than later something had to give and it was only a matter of time before they both would figure out the outcome.

CHP 8
"ONE TIME"

After Nesto hit a couple of corners that night, he had plenty of time to think. "Hey Daddy!" The little black girls lost would holler from every corner as he cruised down e 14th St. The night walkers wanted to size up his wallet in exchange for some type of sexual favors. Shit he didn't knock em, but he definitely wouldn't join them especially if it had to do with him reachin in his pocket for it. That was for sure a no-no. The way of life on the streets was undoubtably riskyand was like a game of russian roulette. In the streetz you had to move mean or you were just better off staying in the house. At certain hours of the night, the streetz were filled with opportunities depending on what type of game you had and type of product or services that you had to offer. But you definitely had no room for error. By the time Nesto got to 82nd ave he made a left, when he saw the police cruiser following him. The dick heads had nuthin better to do than to fuck wit a nigga in a clean ass whip, especially as clean as his. When he got to Plymouth St, he made a right turn to see if they were really on him, and they were. They turned on their lights and you could hear them clearly on the loud horn as they directed him. "Pull over and turn the car off" one of the dickheads said. The driver got out and and proceeded with caution as he made his way up to the window. "License and registration" he said. The other officer approached the passenger side shortly, flashing the light inside of the car hoping to see some incriminating evidence. Nesto reached in his pocket for his wallet and pulled out his california drivers license along with the papers that frank had left him in the glove box. "Just bought the car im assuming?" As the officer took a thorough examination of the paperwork. "Yea, yesterday as a matter of fact" Nesto replied "you on parole or probation?" The officer asked "no sir" he told them knowing that the only thing that would possibly show up in the computer would be that he was out on bail. "Hold on a sec" he said as he walked back to his car to run the info. Nesto knew that if they wanted to be dicks they could take him in right now just for coming into contact with the police, so his heart was damn near ready to jump out of his chest. When he looked at dickhead number two he just looked like he had nothin better to do and would love to take himstraight to the eastmont sub-station for the pettiest shit they could find. When the officer returned he said "is there anything in the car that we should know about?" "No sir" Nesto replied humbl ready to get it all over with. The police had been actin brand new every since four officers got murdered last year a block away from eastmont mall. "Step out the car please!" He said. "Your all the way on the other side of town and were just wondering what business you have going on out here this late" the officer inquired. "Yea I just got done dropping my kids off, or do you think all we do is ride around and smoke weed all day?" Nesto roared mad that he had gotten inconvienenced. "Shut the fuck up" dickhead #2 shouted "yea, whatever!" Nesto roared angrily realizing that this was starting to go too far. "Oooogghh! Whats this?" The dickhead said and held up a ziplock bag full of white powder. "You know you are in a red flag zone known for high drug activity right?" Dickhead number #2 said with a evil grin on his face. "Look that shit aint mi—" and before he could get all the words out of his mouth dickhead #1 shoved his billy club right into Nesto's stomach hard enough to knock the wind out of his body" shut the fuck up, we don't wanna hear no sad stories. The officer protested. "Oh we are just full of surprises tonight arent 'we?" Dickhead #2 said as he held up another bag with what looked like to be a nine millimeter hand gun. "Come on man, why yall tryin to fuck me over" he pleaded "wham!!!" Dickhead #1 gave Nesto another solid blow to the stomach that buckled him next to the car. "Cuff em" one of the dicks said. As soon as the officer reached down to pick him up they got a call over the dispatch. "We have a possible 211 in progress in the 900 block of Birch St . . . 3 Males with black hoodies . . . Possibly armed and dangerous" "you got lucky this time motherfucker! Don't let us see your black ass out here again tonight or you won't be so lucky." The officer saidas he dropped nestos id and paperwork on the ground right next to him, and just like that they were gone. After Nesto got his self together he picked his shit up and hopped back into his whip and got the fuck up out of there. After he hit a couple of corners he was back on 82nd ave and followed it all the way up to the freeway to get the fuck up outta the east. Shit like this happened everyday and trust me it was alot of cats sitting in jail right now because of crooked muthafuckas like them. Nesto hit Finesse on the mobile to find out where he was. "Brah" he said as Finesse picked up onthe first ring. "Sup wit it" Finesse asked "shit just got jacked sky high by one time and them dirty muthafuckas tried to put a gun **and** some dope on me!" Nesto told him, still heated about the situation. "Man you already know these crooked muthafuckaz aint playin fair" he said "where you at" Nesto said trying to get finesses location. "Shit, kinda tied up right now trying to get the rest of my meal from earlier" he shot back in code. It was obvious that he had hooked up with baby from earlier and most likely he was trying to knock that down. "Aight dog imma hit you in the morning, we gotta hook up." Nesto said "aight just hit me!"

As soon as the conversation was over Nesto hit end on the phone, it had been a long day and he was about ready to get outta the streetz before he got caught up. After he came up with a destination, he hit his boy Rick to see what was crackin. Nesto knew Rick was up fa show cuz this was the time that he usually got off work. It was about one o clock in the morning and he picked up right as Nesto got to west Oakland and came over the downtown ramp to the 27th street exit. "Hello?" Rick answered kinda cranky "wussup my nigg" Nesto said happy to get through "who dis?" "Nesto fool, you don't recognize my voice no more I ain't been gone that long" "oh boy, I didn't know who this was and plus yo ass becallin from so many different numbers how was I suppose to know?" "It's kool, ahy im about to be pullin up in the back so open the door." "Shit im already outside nephew, im sittin in da stang." Rick was like a big brother to Nesto, because he always knew the right things to do at the right times . . . . He would never sugar coat nothin for nobody . . . . He was the truth!" All he ever talked about was money and weed and getting his little brother back. He was so fascinated with weed that he always had so many different strands to sample. When Nesto pulled up Rick was sittin in his mustang. That car was a certified bread winner and if need be would give the five-o a run for their money. Nesto had seen it in action too may times before. Nesto respected big bro Rick so much because he had seen him come from the bottom to the top. Talkin bout no help, homeless, sleepin in his bucket, to holdin down his job for like probably the last ten years, flipped his own spot and upgraded the bucket to a 4.6 Nesto pulled in on the Sycamore St. Side into the parking lot and parked right next to him. "Wassup you black ass nigga" Rick said "where the fuck you been at?" He added. Rick used to date one of nestos girl cousins back in the day, not to mention Nesto used to live like right around the corner. Nesto would practically live at his house when him and the baby mamaz would get into it. "Shit I just got out" Nesto told him with a serious face, and I damn near just went back fuckin wit dem shady ass dickheads out there in the east." Nesto said. "Shit, you already know how shit be, you betta be kool" Rick said like he was the coolest nigga in cali. "I got too much love for you Nesto to see you go out on some fake ass shit, you gotta be more careful famm!" Nesto took a minute to reflect and then agreed. "See this shit right here!! . . . . This will make you forget all about that" he said as he pulled out the weed he had got from the cannabais club. "Dis shit right here!! . . . . Dis shit right hear nigga" he said laughing like crazy doing his katt williams impression. "Will give you a head high" Rick said "but this shit right here as he pointed to another strand, will give you a body high" Rick carried on. "Nigga you did always think you was the dean edell of weed . . . Dr. Oz or some fuckin body" Nesto said "Nigga . . . N-e-wayz . . . . We bout to roll em both up" Rick insisted as he passed Nesto a swisher sweet to gut. "You talked to Nelly" Rick asked, as he inquired about nestos cuzzin. "Nah I aint got a chance to slide through there, I was about to make rounds, but the dickheads threw rain on my parade" he babbled on. "Shit, you be aight!" He said laughing trying to put some humor inthe situation. They chopped it up for a couple of more minutes, as they had finished rolling up the weed. Rick stayed in the baby jet, this muthafucka used to be like new jack city back in the day, it had calmed down a whole lot since then. As they were about to enter the building it was some tweakers that were coming from the top of the stairs looking like they had just took a mac blast of that good shit. "Got some blow . . . Got some crack . . . . Wussup?" The dengy old woman with one lucky tooth in her mouth asked. Her jeans were covered with filth like she had just come from underneath somebodies car giving an oil change "nah, you don't need no more dope auntie . . . . You need a bath 4real . . . Take yo dusty ass on somewhere we ain't got nuthin for ya!!" Rick said as they kept it movin inside. Rick and Nesto must of rolled up like three more chops after the first two were gone and played a couple of games on the playstation 3. "Shit you lookin like new money wit dat wet ass ss outside, what type of moves you been makin tobe so fresh out. "Some of my old school work put me on wit dat paper game, and me and Nesse been doing a couple of jobs." Shit I been debating whether or not I wanna get back in the game "Nesse told him while he waited for his opinion." Look, imma tell you like this, and this is cause I love you bruh . . . . You need to find you a job, you got yo kids depending on you and at the same time by no means am I telling you to be a poor hustler. Im just trying to tell you that whatever you choose to do just be smart about it. Come on now, you know "aint no love in this town." Be smart because the odds are already against you and it was designed to keep the black man down" he protested. "This nigga need to be somebody motivational speaker" Nesto thought to himself. "Just look at me lil bruh, aint nobody ever gave me nuthin! Everything I wanted I had to go and get it. It ain't like im telling you nuthin you don't know. You got the game but what is you gon do wit it? You wanna be out here in the town running these streetz forever or do you wanna be able to get you and yo family out the ghetto and go live like dem white niggas? Man dats somethin for you to think about. Im confident that you will make the right decision . . . . And with that said . . . . My nigga do you!! . . . But be smart!!!" And after that Nesto heard what he needed to hear. Everything he said after that point was a blurr, because he had his mind made up . . . . Just one more time!!.

CHP 9
THE BIGGER "THE WEIGHT THE BIGGER THE STAKES"

When Nesto awoke the next day he had everything figured out. He thought to himself how this all had turned into a game of chess and he knew how to play very well. He figured since every good army had a five star lieutenant, he would have to figure out who that was going to be . . . . It was time to push some pawns. Neither Nesto nor ness could afford to go down, so they had to play the backfield, push some pieces, and attack when necessary. Nesto called up his boy Stacks and told him to get dressed because he would be by there to get him. For the record Nesto and Stackz went way back, and as far as he knew, Stackz was a solid dude that hugged a little paper from time to time, on a consistent basis. He lived in the high rises, which was some projects in the heart of west Oakland. Nesto knew that if he gave Stackz the ball, he would know exactly what to do wit it. Running coke was never really Stackz thing, he liked to play with heroin . . . but given the opportunity to see some real money fucking with the coke, Nesto knew he wouldn't turn it down. Nesto and Finesse used to hustle over there back in the day, so they knew that it was money over there. There definitely was a whole lot of action to go wit it too . . . so the operation had to have some structure. Nesto got to Stackz about 8 in the morning and picked him up at the store on 8th and adeline. They rode all the way to the other side of town to the oaks club to have breakfast. "So wasup Nesto? . . . I know dis betta have something to do with some raw dollaz . . . wakin da kid up at dese wee hours of the mornin"!! Stackz said, rubbing is hands together anxiously. "You know wassup brah, you know im business" Nesto assured him. It was time for everybody to eat, and come up at the same time. The most important part was keeping it solid all the way around and nobody feeling like they were getting the short end of the stick. Nesto had to see if he was game and if he felt like he was up for the challenge. "This street shit could be a real headache sometimes." He thought to himself, so he wasted no time getting to the point. "Look" he said looking Stackz straight in the eyes . . . "Me and Nesse been thinkin bout getting this shit rollin again, and we aint talkin bout pushing no peanuts . . . Ya hear me?" "If you aint wit da shit . . . and really ready to get down wit the crown . . . then don't even put ya feet down . . . Cuz it ain't no straddlin the fence . . . either you in or you out . . . Simple as that!!" Nesto summed it all up, and quickly scanned the room. They tried to keep a low profile, as people were just starting to come in from either a long night of gambling on those card tables or just checkin in for that early morning cup of coffee and perhaps something to eat. The oaks club was were alot of game players met up to conduct business . . . from soliciting girls to moving packages . . . Everybody was suspect from the blacks to the asians. "Im in!" Stackz said, as he returned the eye contact. "I need you to get your soldiers together then . . . We got a couple of days before we touch down with this work . . . im talkn bout pillz, weed, and coke. No lttle shit my man, we about to be moving some major weight . . . And you already know the bigger the weight the bigger the stakes." Nesto concluded . . .

"Man Nesto on my mamma . . . you know im da nigga to move mean or you wouldn't have even got back wit me in the first place" Stackz said with much confidence. "The oaks club was filled with so many beautiful eritrean looking women, walking by giving them eye contact . . . It was kinda hard for them to fully concentrate . . ." Like I said . . . Stackz paused . . . . Then looked back at Nesto after watching a big juicy ass, that caught his eye, walk to the back of the resturant. "I move mean baby . . . . You think im tryin to be out here starvin like the rest of these niggas? . . . I don't think so!! . . . . Well lets eat then!" Nesto meant that in every aspect of the interpretation . . . as soon as ness's man got back to him with the price of them chickens, they would be ready to move. Nesto already had everything else lined up but with so much on the line . . . . He did have to go and check one more trap. They were definitely going to need some artillery, because when that money started rolling in, niggaz was gone hate and think they could just take shit. Nobody made the rules, because there were none. Nesto knew that to well . . . along with everybody else that stepped on the concrete in the streetz of Oakland . . . . In the dope game . . . . If you weren't going to try to master it, then why risk your life playing? That was the way that Nesto always seen it. By the time they finished up their meal, Nesse had hit Nesto on the horn "ehy boy were you at?" Nesse spoke as he pondered aimlessly when Nesto picked up the other line. "Shit just about to leave the oaks club and take Stackz back to the highrises. Im just wrappin up with him so let me hit you back in a min." Nesto told em. "Aight!" Ness agreed. And hung up. It only took Nesto about 10 minutes to get Stackz back to his crib. "Get yourself together brah, mentally and physically" Nesto told em "and be ready to move in a couple of days . . . As soon as I get the green light imma let you know" he assured Stackz. As Stackz got out the car Nesto told em "it just got real don't fuck me!" "Its good" Stackz reassured Nesto and gave him a pound, slammed the door and then was gone. When Nesto hit Nesse back, Nesse told him that he was in the east and to meet him up the street from the infamous 69th St village. He was at one of the homies house about to get his haircut. Nesto slipped in and out of the lanes letting the high performance kit work its magic as he shifted gears pushing to the east. "Damn I love this car" he thought as he smiled to himself. He turned up the music and rolled up the windows, as he kept his foot on the gas . . . Doing it moving . . . Pushing through traffic . . . . "Rah-rah!, Rah-rah!" . . . He got greeted with a million growls . . . Nesto had much respect from his loved ones as he pulled up to the spot. He could hear everyboby ranting and raving . . . Like they hadn't seen that nigga in years. "Nesto wasup?" Dinosaur said "nigga we heard you been dancin around the town in your new whip and shit . . . . Cutting up!!" Dinosaur said as he gave Nesto his props. "Shit . . . You know da kid stay fresh" Nesto said "just trying to organize some crime so we can leave these streetz to the next generation of crazy ass youngstas. Dinosaur was an old school homie, a straight classic. He was the barber to the underground. This nigga was so raw that he didnt need no shop, he just cut hair right out of his house and on his back porch . . . Not to mention he was the michael vick of Oakland as well . . . He was known for breeding pitts, him and his brother dyno baby. The click was all family and were connected for years. They got tight when all of them were going to school and working at the east bay conservation corps. Them dudes went to work loaded everyday . . . And was on the clock getting paid for it . . . Nesto thought of how they used to go out to different areas and knock out acres of grass and trees, clean trenches, and all types of crazy shit for minimum wage. "Rah!-Rah! . . . . Rah!-Rah!" Nesto jumped out the car and gave all the soldiers a fist pound to exchange the love . . . "Where the fuck you been at my nigga?" Orange asked "man you already know" Nesto said "yea we figured that" killa g added, as they made their way to the back of the house. It was about two niggas already waiting to get cut and Nesse was already in the chair. Nesto seen his boy R.B another old school homie that was just hangin out chillin. "Da whole famm out today huh?" Nesto said as he entered into the midst of the chaos. Finesse was telling everybody how he had the lil waitress bitch doing all type of little strange shit last night "nah . . . But fa-real she was holding it like she was auditioning for american idol or some shit" he said clearly just acting a fool. "A nigga went hollywood yall . . . Man fa realz" Nesse said as he continued to do the fool. "She was looking like this when I gave it to her" and he made that face that was on the mask of the killer in scary movie . . . . Nesse could be a real classic character sometimes, when it came to cracking on somebody. He was clearly the center of attention, it was some type of swag that he had about himself that made people just wanna listen to him . . . After dinosaur finished up on nesses hair Nesto hopped in the chair right behind him . . . In total disregard of anybody else and just started running it in. "Man, so who ready to get this money?" Nesto said taking total control of the moment. "Shit who ain't ready to get this money?" Dyno baby said as he looked around smiling. Nesto ran down the whole plan and by the time he was finished everybody was all ears and ready to get active. After they had spent a few racks on the whips, $2400.00 On chains, $3 racks on the clothes, $600.00 On phones plus the "g" that Nesto gave to his baby mama they had about twenty-five racks left to play with. Shit they were damn near broke "hold on let me take this call" Nesse said as he spunt off away from the crowd. He returned in a couple of minutes with the news that he had just got from nitty . . . "17.5 Dawg" . . . He said. Everybody pretty much knew what he was talkin about . . . that wasn't too bad at all considering that it was a drought going on rite now and the price could have been turnt all the way up. They had learned through the years that it was really about who you knew. That high priced shit was for them suckaz to pay . . . "Listen up everybody" Nesto said, hoping that everybody heard exactly what he had to say. "Now all of us trying to eat, and we will . . . . The only thing is that we are coming from the bottom to the top so we need every red penny . . .

Now we only got about twenty-five racks left to play with so . . . lets just get to the numbers". Nesto seen niggaz already counting shit up on they fingerz "listen up Nesto ordered . . . We got enough for one kick(a kilo of coke), 2 boats of ecstasy pillz . . . Which was a total of 2,000 pillz, that we are getting for a dollar a piece wholesale . . . We can give them away for five dollars each . . . . Which would bring us back a total of eight thousand dollars from the two boats every time we flip. Then last but not least . . . we have forty-two hundred left to spend on the dro . . . Which would get us two p's. If we sold qps only we could turn over 3 racks profit off the weed easily . . . Nesto had it all mapped out and after the meeting they all had a solid agreement and everybody in attendance knew exactly what it was . . . .

CHP 10
THE START OF A DYNASTY

The very next day, Nesto called Lollipop to see what was going on, on her side. She told him that she was putting together one of her yearly trips to Miami, Florida. If he didn't know any better he would think it was a regular vacation but . . . He did know better . . . She was on her way out there to run some more of that paper. Nesto was for sure that he wasn't about to be left out after the bank roll she put him up with . . . Off the first couple of licks. Nesto told Lollipop that if she could afford to front him and Nesse's tickets, they would fly down there and make a couple of more runs with her. She told him that it was cool as long as they could slide her cheese back because her mortgage payment was right around the corner. Now that they finally had shit ready to rock on the streets, it was definitely about keeping shit lined up. They left Stackz with all the work they had talked about and came to the conclusion that he was going to be the middle man between them and the drug trades. Lollipop said the itinerary confirmed the flight to be leaving out of sfo next week on thursday, early in the morning, and it was about a thirteen hour flight . . . They only had one lay over in atlanta so they should be arriving in Miami later on that night. Nesto never did too much traveling, so he was lookin forward to getting of out the town. "I know Nesse is about to go skitz when he founds out what I got lined up for us" Nesto thought to himself. After Nesto and Nesse fronted all the money for the shit, they only had about thirteen hundred dollars left. Nesto took his seven hundred dollars, put it up and gave the rest to Nesse. Trying to think ahead, he thought, right now would be the time to start putting some chips up just to be prepared in case anything unexpectedly happened. After they got played the first time, by that shady ass lawyer, Nesto figured they would be better off stacking bail money. This was mandatory business. They did pretty good for the first run, it took them a couple of weeks to run off all that work, and get the clientele restablished. When they did that first pick up, they had made all the money back that they spent on the coke alone, not to mention over an extra 36 racks to the corner pocket. That was damn near 40 racks in profit that they were pulling back and that was pretty damn good. By the time the next week came and it was time to leave, shit . . . They were kicking back, sipping lemonade . . . Stackz was running major work out the high rises and making drops between east and west Oakland and berkeley. He was a "hustla fa show" and they had no regrets behind putting their manz on! Stackz was to run the operation and keep them posted with how shit was moving back in the town . . . until they touched back down!!

CHP 11
"GOTTA EAT EVEN THOUGH WE ATE"

Nesto waited until the day before they were scheduled to leave before him and Nesse met up with the connect to re-up. This would give them plenty of time to go out of town and do their thing with Lollipop before they needed to recopp again. Once they got rid of the work from the first run, Nesse and Nesto was able to find a little flat in East Oakland off fruitvale ave and e 27th street. It was a cool spot because there was definitely alot of traffic around and for the price of the rent, you couldn't beat it for a two bedroom . . . There was las palmas, which was the talk of the town for their famous shrimp burritos and seafood, everette and jones bbq, a nail shop, a liquor store and a metro phone store right there and they stayed in the middle of it all and caught a close up on everythang moving . . . Nesse had met this chick named raisun, in the area, that was hella cool . . . Nesto thought how Nesse must have really been feeling her because . . . He hadn't seen him that much since they moved there. Nesse was obviously spending most of his time at her house. She had three kids and two little sisters named jamaica and shawna. When Nesto got back to the house, after making a few rounds, he seen Finesse sitting in the coupe with raisun "toot!!!-Toot!!!" His horn blared as he switched gears to slow down, and park right of them. When he got out of the car, he put up the peace sign and then his index finger to motion that he would be right back. He ran over to las palmas right quick to put in his order for one of their famous shrimp burritos. As he made his way through the door, if he didn't see a chick with a body like "buffy the body" the video vixen and a face like halle berry, then he guessed he just hadent seen shit . . . At least not in Oakland . . . It was real . . . She was real and damn . . . this girl was bad as hell. "Nesto thought to himself all the while unable to take his eyes off her . . ." "Wasup mommaz?" Nesto spoke, trying not to keep his cool and giving her a seductive look . . . "Hello" she said as she turned slightly towards him as if she had been waiting on him to speak . . . she had on some red and yellow rimmed christian dior glasses, a red flowery sundress that showed off every little bit of curve that her ass had to offer and some and some red and yellow wedge heel sandals with perfectly french manicured toes. "You in line?" Nesto asked, trying to make a little small talk . . . "I already ordered" she replied giving him a seductive look up and down . . . Shit . . . Why wouldn't she be on him too . . . He thought . . . He had his gear on today too . . . Some black rocawear jeans, a coke white t-shirt, some black and white blazers on his feet and not to mention all his gold jewelry that complimented his skin tone . . . He felt black and gold was just the look for him . . . "How can I make that phone ring" he playfully said pointing to the I-phone she held on to for dear life, that must have rang like a thousand times since they had been in the resturant . . . "Excuse me?" She said curiously in a prissy voice "I said . . . How can I make that phone ring too" Nesto said once more persistently stepping closer to her . . . She turned around, made direct eye contact and said . . . "Yo money ain't long enough, you might wanna try one of these low-budget hoes" and waved her hand around at all the other young stallions that were waiting amongst them . . . "Bitch you got me fucked up" one of the girls yelled out in protest . . . Not feeling her cockiness. "Please!" She said arrogantly, and rolled her neck around. "Come on ma, I know a lil sumthin about christian dior, a lil sumthin about the stick in the floor, about a lil prada, a lil dolce & gabbana. Im just sayin give a gangsta a chance . . . she looked hella prissy but Nesto could tell that she had some street in her from the knowledge of the lyrics he had just spit to her off the boy boy's messy marv album . . . "Are you always this charming?" She asked . . . Seemingly giving in . . . "I couldn't tell you because . . . I don't run into beautiful girls like you everyday" Nesto shot back . . . She started to switch gears as she began to brief him about her business . . . She explained how she couldn't figure out which one turned her on more the sex or the money . . . "Within a short time ive matured, and I know its work . . . It's business . . . The sex . . . The fame" she said putting him up to speed to where her head was at. "Im a grown ass woman and ain't nobody gonna take care of me better than me . . . So I gotta handle my business . . . I gotta get paid because there is too much money to be made out here" she continued. "Now that im on my own, im always on tour doing signings, features, private parties, directing, and meeting with investors that are coming up with new projects." She had a whole lot to stay in those few minutes and was sure enough something else. "Sounds like you stay pretty busy and don't have time for a man" Nesto asked trying to get some insides . . . Hoping that she would correct him. "Naw, I don't have a man right now because im tied up between what I want and need . . . I can't handle or commit to anything right now . . . Except for making money . . ." I honestly do kinda want one though, it just takes a certain kind of man to handle my situation . . . someone ultimately secure with himself . . . Sometimes I feel that because I am so independent . . . That men can't do anything for me except let me bust a super fat nut in his mouth" . . . She explained with a wink . . . "Wooooow" was all Nesto could say, surprised by her choice of words. "Order 72!" The tiny asian woman behind the window hollered. "That's me" she said as she grabbed her order and slowly stepped outside hoping to continue their conversation. She went on to tell him all about her favorite positions and how she loved to pretend she was a cow girl and sit on the dick backwards. "Oh my god that makes me cum so hard because I love feeling the dick hit this one spot." She said closing her eyes as if she was feeling it right then . . . Nesto knew either she had a really good sex game or one hell of a imagination . . . Whichever one it was, Nesto was about to make it his business to figure it out . . . He could see Nesse and raisun still sitting across the street and they now had their attention focused on Nesto and his prime rib piece of meat that stood looking him in his face. "You know a chick that loves twisting in the sheets will always have a popping social life . . . . but when a woman makes an effort to have really connected sex involving both the body and the mind . . . She goes from a good girlfriend, to wifey material from my point of view" Nesto lectured . . . As he tried to lace her up on something real. "Men long for sex that makes them feel deeply bonded . . . In other words . . . It's not only about how far you can put your legs behind your neck . . . The most important part about having a big booty is paying close attention to our mind sets and mood during the session . . . So sex reaches a higher, almost spiritual level" Nesto concluded, as she nodded in agreement the whole time. "Number 81!" The tiny asian woman screamed out once more. "That's me" Nesto said "well you know I really enjoyed our conversation . . . I wouldn't mind hearing from you from time to time, do you have a number?" She asked. "Do I?" Nesto replied both anxiouslyand sarcastically. "Are you gonna do somethin wit it . . . Is the question" Nesto added in smoothly. "Yea, give it to me" she said aggressively. "Damn . . . Right here, right now on the street" he asked laughing, putting a major smile on her face . . . After they exchanged numbers she said "you don't even know my name" "what is it? Nesto replied. "Nadia . . . But you can just call me naughty!!" She said as she licked her glossy lips and made her way to her car, a cherry red BMW 3 series, black on black tint, with stock alloyd rims. Nesto just stood there in amazement of how she could just flaunt her swagg around so nonchalantly. As far as he was concerned, he had just knocked one of the badest bitches ever and the cold part about it was, she wasn't even from Oakland . . . Not even from california for that matter. He ran in to get his food and shot back across the street so he could eat and finish getting his things together for the run tomorrow. They had an early flight and Nesto knew that he needed to get some rest. Nesse and raisun were still at it. It was as if they had met in a past life because it seemed they had so much to talk about. Nesto and Nesse's poor little apartment was naked. It looked like a trap house because there was no furniture or anything else in the house. That was only minor though, because as soon as they got back, Nesto had already planned to have Ms. Naughty come and help do some interior decorating. Nesto just sat on the floor and just laughed as he thought about her. After he was halfway done with his burrito Nesse came bursting into the house "dog who was that?" He said "you like that huh?" Nesto said. "That was nadia the newest to my collection" he said talking like she was an article of clothing, a pair of shoes or a trophy. "You really poppin huh?" He said laughing trying to get out all of his sillyness. "I mean yall was talkn for about an hour, she probably mad that her foods cold noww" he said continuing on with the sillyness. "She'll be aight," Nesto said as continued to finish his off. "So you ready for Miami?" Nesse asked, obviously excited about the trip just as much as Nesto was. "Lollipop said that we would run the paper the same way that we did the first time, just in another state this time. I'm pretty sure we will have plenty of leisure time too" Nesto informed him. Nesto wandered if Moco was coming along but thought out loud "you tell me sherlock, you the one having menage' trois and shit" Nesse said cheesing . . . "Oh yea" Nesto said replaying the scene and cracking up inside about the whole situation. They both made eye contact and just started laughing. "I told raisun she could come too . . ." Nesse said watching Nesto's reaction . . . I know you didn't tell her that she could come . . . You know . . . we going to take care of some serious business right" Nesto asked no longer smiling. "She cool man, she down . . . I been checkin her out, she solid . . . Don't worry about it" Nesse assured. "Damn . . . Nigga you sprung already" Nesto asked "so what" he shot back smiling. "Well . . . at least you ain't in denial about the shit" Nesto said . . . "Yea far from it" he announced "well if you like it . . . then I love it" Nesto said and that was that. "Im bout to go tell her to pack her bags" Nesse said jokingly. "Get yo little sprung ass outta here" Nesto pretended a kicking motion, as he shot out the door. It is said, god puts people together for a reason and we will find out about raisun later on, Nesto thought to himself. Nesto finished up with everything that he needed to do and decided to waste some time catching up on the games he hardly ever had the time to play on his x box 360. He chose grand theft auto 4 because he needed to get the feel for the game again since it had been so long since he played. Nikko bellia, fresh off the boat from europe hoped he could escape his past. His cousin roman, planned that together they could find fortune in liberty city. As they slip into debt and were dragged into the criminal underworld by a series of shiesters, thieves, and psychopaths, they discover that life isn't as sweet as they thought. Its a city that worships money and status, and is a haven for those who have it and a living nightmare for those who didn't. Nesto loved that game. After he played a couple of games on the x box, Nesse was finally making his way back in with raisun right behind him. Shit who did they think they were bonnie and clyde or bobby and whitney? . . . raisun had her bags all packed "oh my god" she said excitedly "I never been to Miami! I bet you the water out there is so beautiful . . . she had a vibe about her that was really outgoing, so Nesto didn't really mind her being around. He was tired and definitely about to get him some z's, wasnt really up for the chit-chat. He left Nesse and raisun in the living room because there was only one T.V in the house, dragged his air mattress to his room and faded to black . . . All alone.

CHP 12
A TRIP TO SOUTHBEACH

By 745 am, Nesto, Nesse, raisun, and lolloipop were on a first class flight to mi-yayo. Nesse told raisun if they couldn't get her on one of the early flights out with them, they would just let her drive back and hold the whip until they got back . . . luckily, they were able to get a seat due to someone cancelling at the last minute. This was Nesto's second time on a plane and he was really enjoying the presidential view of the world as he watched the plane move over land, water and through so many clouds. The stewardess had just given strict instructions on what to do in case of an emergency, as she robotically chimed "have a great flight and thank you for flying southwest. Nesto and Lollipop had seats parrallel to each other, while Nesse and raisun had to work something out with some guy that was flying alone. "So what's up" Lollipop said asking curiously to find out exactly what Nesto had been up to. "You act like you don't know a bitch no more huh . . . Cuz . . . You know . . . I been missin you like crazy!" Lollipop added with a little bit of humor. Lollipop was kool but the relationship between her and Nesto, in his mind, was basically a toss up, because he felt, it could never be anything else. Lollipop was cool and the sex game was crazy, but as far as the their personalities were concerned, he felt they werent compatible so Nesto saw the shit for what it was, and didn't try to take it any further. All they could ever be was fuck buddies and hustlin partners . . . That's it. "You know I been thinking Nesto, maybe you should really give us a chance . . . . We a good look boo, plus we out here getting money and you already know that fucking with me . . . you ain't gone have to want for nuthin or nobody for that matter!" Lollipop said seriously trying to convince him that she was the truth. "Wait a minute now . . . I'm really just tryin to stay focused right now baby, because I got so much shit going on." Nesto said as he shot down her vision. Nesto and Nesse had just gotten back in the game and if they didn't stay focused, there would be consequences and repercussions that neither of them were ready to deal with. Nesto ran it down to Lollipop the best way he knew how, because, shit, at the same time that's just how it really was at the moment. "You know you still my number one draft pick though right?" Nesto told her as he lied, trying to silently stroke her ego and make up for his nonchalantness. He knew as of right now though, he had to be focused and nothing else really mattered except getting that money. He knew who his number one draft pick really was and even though he knew she was solid . . . He didn't have Lollipop in mind. It was "naughty nadia" and Nesto couldn't wait to swoop throught the adult store, so he could catch up with her movie collection and see if she was really all that she claimed to be. Only time would tell about that one. "I might hit that before I actually hit that!" Nesto thought to himself as he let off a grin that really said a million words. "Well you know that im 100% behind you Daddy in whatever you decide to do . . . . I just love you so much and want to see everything work out for you Nesto!" Lollipop said now feeling rejected and trying to hide her tear filling eyes. "I know baby" Nesto said after a couple of minutes, trying to refocus on the conversation after thinking about nadia. They finally cleared everybody to use their phones and any other type of electronics that were available. Nesto called Stackz "top of the morning my nigga" Nesto said when he heard Stackz the pick up the phone. "Hey what's good?" Stackz said. "Aw you know just callin to check on you bruh" Nesto informed him "what it's lookin like? Nesto asked curiously." "Everything is movin as planned, and going smooth . . . . I told you don't worry man I got this." Stackz said, tryin to reassure Nesto that he had made the right decision in leaving him with all the work. Nesto looked back at Finesse and gave him a thumbs up to let him know everything was everything. It was something about airplanes that just made Nesto sleepy. Raisun was already knocked out in her seat with her face glued to the glass window and Nesse was reading a king magazine that he had picked up from the airport. "So wasup with ya girl Moco?" When she gone let us slide through that bank that she work at?" Nesto asked Lollipop. "You know it's funny that you said that because she said that they don't be treating her right up there and she was thinking about quitting. "You know she been up there for about five years and them crackerz still aint been giving her, her raises ontime". Lollipop said "well you tell her that the team is back together and we need some work" Nesto said as he played his trumph cards and giving her a grimmacing look at the same time. "You ain't sad nuthin but a word" she shot back returning the look they chit-chatted for about another hour or so, before their eyes rolled to the back of their heads. Nesto was tired and since he had been home from jail, he had grown accustomed to sleeping in again. He woke up and fell asleep about ten times before they actually had to switch planes in atlanta. About eight hours later they were dropping out of the sky finally in Miami. It had gotten dark really fast so they could tell they were in another time zone.

Miami was definitely the show. As soon as they touched down, they caught a cab to the hotel where they had reservations. It was right across the street from the beach on the famous ocean blvd. They passed up versace's house on the way there, it was a big ass mansion right on the strip. They really had a nice view of the beach from their suite. Everything was top of the line. The room had a flat screen T.V hanging on the wall, a king sized bed with the mirrors on the ceiling, an in-room jacquzzi, and a kitchen with everything that they would need for their stay including a washer and dryer. The living room had nice exotic animals such as leopards and lions statues blending in with the furniture. The balcony with its sliding glass doors took you straight out to the beach. There were lounge chairs and even a table outside for night time dining. They could tell that the night life was off the chain because eventhough it was darkoutside it was still hot and everybody was out having a good time in their sandals and flip-flops. The weather was like none other, definitely a complete difference from california. It just didn't happen in cali like that unless you were in sacramento or pittsburg somewhere. As soon as they got settled in, they hit ocean blvd to get a tour of the city, and the things that it had to offer. They stopped at this one joint called "wet willies" and had a couple of drinks and something to eat. They had this one drink called "call me a cab" and that was exactly what you needed to do by the time you finished the drink. The drinks in Miami had twice the liquor of regular drinks hidden in them and was sure to have you drunk as a sailor tryin to get back to land. They browsed alot of the shoppping stores and souvenir shops. Lollipop practically made a list of all the stores and shops that she seen that they would pay a second visit tomorrow. They were standing in front of some bar called "the pearl" when they seen "lil wayne" cruising down the strip in a yellow lamborghinni with the doors up, and his cup of lean. This was where all the ballers took a trip when they needed to get away. They all walked across the street to the beach and got comfortable looking at the waves push up on to the sand. There was a party going on . . . . Music . . . . Bon-fires . . . . And a whole lot of alcohol. They all thought of how it seemed that these people ever went to sleep. It seemed as though they had so much fun that they didn't know what sleep was, and if they did decide to sleep, they would go no further than where they already were. The people were so friendly and happy to see other couples that they invited Nesse and Nesto along with the girls to chill with them at the bon-fire. Lollipop pulled out her secret stash and they rolled up about six sticks. Raisun didn't smoke so Finesse kept her full of lemon drops and mai-tai's. By the time they got back to the room they all were good and full. Nesto and Lollipop made their own little bon-fire with the mosh pit they had on the balcony and just relaxed in the lawn chairs. After they finished the drinks they had brought back with them they passed out.

They woke up at sunrise. Lollipop asked Nesto to go with her to get a rental car so they could get around. She said that one of her friends was throwing a pleasure party tonight and wanted them all to come. It took them about an hour to get to the car rental spot. All they had was exotic shit, and premium coupes, which Nesto thought was a gimmick fareal. They wanted everybody spending top dollars while you were there. Nesto thought to himself again that damn . . . This was where all the ballerz came to play in their leisure time. After being convinced, Lollipop took the maserati granturismo which was expensive and heavy but indeniably beautiful, sensuous and as italian as the leaning tower of babel. Out of all of the options a BMW m3, porsche cayman, and the porsche 911, ironically, the maserati was the most reasonable in price. After all, they had came here to make money not spend it, but at the same time shit, you only had one time to live like this right? At least that was how Lollipop felt. By the time they had got back to the suite Finesse and raisun were already dressed. They had just gotten back from getting raisun something to wear. She had on a bad two-piece versace skirt and halter set that truly complimented her exotic frame, Nesto knew that Nesse had made a beneficial investment.

After they hit all the stores and banks, they could find going into the city, they called it a day. By the time the sun fell out of the sky, they had a pocket full of money, plenty of clothes, jewelry, and whatever else they wanted. They ended up making this a bad habit. It was the first, but hopefully not the last time, they would venture off on a platinum business trip like this one. The first day they got around to all the stores and souvenir shops, so the next day they drove into the city, but this time they left Nesse and raisun at the room. "How you feelin about mi-yayo?" Lollipop asked "this definitely is the limelight" Nesto said as he turned to look her in the eyes. He felt like a boss when Rick ross's "speeding" came on the radio, because that's exactly what they were doing . . . . Speeding through this city and reaping all the benefits they could before they got on that plane back to Oakland. There was money to be made out there and the plan was in motion. "What you lookin like on that work?" She asked "well we straight for now. The machine is moving and we got all our men in place. It's just a process sometimes when your coming from the ground up." Let me tell you we really needed this trip cuz we were down to our last." Nesto said "hey, thats what friends are for" Lollipop said smiling happily, glad that she could be of some assistance to him. After a lot of thought and consideration Nesto was really starting to revaluate lollipops position. She was real militant with this money shit and her personality was growing on him, the more time he spent with her. First it was the bail, the paper trail, the menage a trois thing, and now they were having the time of their lives in Miami . . . . What more could a man wish for? Lollipops friends party had gotten postponed until that night because something had came up the previous night. After they hit on a couple of checks, thirty-six to be exact, they had banked up on about thirty-two racks and they still had six days left. The second day Lollipop and raisun went. Lollipop said she was going to put her up on game, since they had been having so much fun together. The third day they all rode out together. After raisun was convinced that she was in, they went back to the rental place and picked up a bugatti veyron which was stupid expensive, but it re-wrote the book on street-car performance. You also had to respect the car had 1001 horsepower to tap on. Nesto and Lollipop swung the maserati to Nesse and raisun, they made it back to the suite with the help from the navigation system. It was a top of the line tom-tom. The gps system had a "M.A.D"(motorist against detection) system built into it. This thing alerted you who when you came up on speedtraps, red light cameras, speed cameras, dui checkpoints and the whole nine. You would receive an audio and video alert everytime you approach an enforcement area. The database contained 23,500 camera locations in the us and canada. They came to the conclusion that the expensive rental cars did have their perks. By the time they split up, they had about eight hours to play with before the party. Nesto and Lollipop were on their way back as Nesto noticed that he had a missed call from his boy Stackz. He had hit him about five times already, not to mention left messages. When he checked his messages Stackz was tellin him about how he needed some more work, because it was rollin so hard that he wanted to go through his own connect to keep things smacking. Nesto immediately felt rage coming over himself from the message, so it was definitely time to give Stackz another call. When the phone answered. "Hey wasup . . . what's the word?" Nesto said "ain't nuthin goin on but the rent baby, shit we ran out of work and now everybody standin out here lookin like some mexicans waitn for work, Stackz said trying to lighten the mood" "well check it don't do anyhting without me. We wrappin up our trip and we should be back within the next two days" Nesto informed him. "Dats too long Nesto! It's money to be ma- . . . . And before he could finish . . ." "Look muthafucka, who run this shit, me or you?" Nesto said ready to snatch Stackz through the phone. Stackz had Nesto pissed. "Who the fuck did Stackz think he was telling him how to run his operation". Nesto thought to himself. "Everything alright baby??" Lollipop inquired "yea everything straight, just a mis-communication" Nesto said. All he knew is that he needed to be smart. One stupid move could cause a tsunami. By the time they all met back up, showered and dressed . . . . They were ready to step out.

CHP 13

When they got to lollipops girlfriends house, it looked like the parking lot of a sold out raiders football game. They saw damn near every car that was was made both in and out of the us. They could hear reggae music, the mellow cries from bob marley could be heard all the way from the street. It took about ten minutes just to get up the winding driveway and absolutely nobody without an invitation was to go through those doors. The all pro, defensive end looking security guard, yielded them in their tracks, as a pretty young thang pranced up to the door. She was wearing a silky looking red bikini with a see through scarf tied around her waist, a chinese jade pendant necklace and a coral and starfish charm bracelet, which was obviously all made by coach. "Come on in" she said seductively greeting Lollipop, damn near putting her tongue down her throat. "This is success" Lollipop said, as she looked backed and winked at the guys . . . "I can see that" Nesto blurted out, cheesing hella hard. "No . . . That's my name silly" . . . The five foot seven, kimmora lee simmons look alike said laughing. She looked as if she was barely twenty one years old. They made it to the ballroom sized living room, where there was a whole entourage of hairstylists, fashion assistants and makeup artists plus a wide variety of friends just mingling and being sociable. It seemed everybody else was there was dancing, having drinks, or tapping away at their iphones. "Make yourself at home" she told the men, as she pushed Lollipop and raisun down into the chairs to get pampered by her own personal prep team. After they were done the prep team had really threw a different face on them . . . from the long lashes, eyebrow waxing and glossy lipsticks, to the america's next top model make up, they were definitely ready to go and walk with the stars. Nesto and Nesse decided to mingle a lil bit and take a tour of the estate. For every second that passed, so did some really hot dames flaunting themselves around half naked. They were defining the true images of "beautiful Miami women" in all shapes, sizes and colors. It was truly so much action and so little drama, that they were not used to it, they were amazed that everybody was actually having a good time. I really could get used to this Nesto said letting his eyes roam the room, "yea . . . No shit" Nesse shot back dazed looking around at the flock of meat following the path Nesto's eyes just took. Every woman they layed eyes on, transformed the floor into a run-way. Even the working men on the payroll had to occassionally abandon their duties and let their lustful eyes run around, pacing the premises. It was so many camera flashes flying through the room, that it looked like a hangout for the papparazzi. They tried to catch every glimpse of the barbie bitches that seductively flaunted themselves through this house, like it was fantasy island or something. When Nesto and Nesse got to the back of the estate, it looked like they were back on the strip. There was a few beachfront mansions that shared the space on the 600 acre piece of land. They finally ran into a couple of grimey, street lookin niggas that were out back smokin a gang of weed . . . "You got some more"? Nesto said referring to the spliff he had rolled up the size of shaq's shoe. "Yaaaaaggggh!" One of them said with some type of jamaican or hatian accent as he arched his back, leaned over and whispered to his buddy in a different language. The dudes were rockin some expensive threads though, shit if it wasn't for the scenery and the accents. They would of swore they were still in the bay area. The dude's buddy left for all of ten minutes, then returned with a grey backpack. "So where arrraaahh you from?" He said. "Da town!," Finesse said quickly filling them in on "Oakland, CA" after they talked to the guys for the next twenty minutes or so, they started to realize that the haitians had the california life fucked up. They thought everybody rode around in low riders hittn switches like snoop dogg in hollywood somewhere. "First of all my man, let me tell you we say "hella" like its going out of style, second of all aint nobody rich . . . Yet . . . Now . . . We still trying to make it up out of the ghetto, and three I know they gotta have a too short or e-40 cd somewhere in this big ass house. Shorty the pimp, born to mac, the dangerous crew? . . . Wassup man . . . What you know about that? Finesse said laughing, as he went off on a tangent. They took a minute for it to register seemingly thinking hard, before it actually registered. "Too short! . . . Yeaahh!!" The one haitian said. The other haitian catted off right along with him and sung the whole first two verses . . . of "freaky tales". Nesto and ness damn near fell to their knees laughing like a muthafucka when they heard them say "freaky tales". That was the proof in the pudding, that shorty the pimp and his freaky tales was definitely internationally known . . . . Biotch! . . . . Shit it didn't take long for the haitians to pick up on the "yay area swag". Fucking with ness and Nesto, swagg points stayed on a million! After they had finished chit-chatting they found out that the two haitians were from lil haiti and from watching episodes of "first 48" Finesse knew that shit was just like "baby bahgdad". "Well . . . I see you guys found some friends" Lollipop said, as her, raisun, and success came strolling outside and joined them in the back. By time the ladies joined them, the smoke was in the air and they were sitting on a cloud. Raisun was peacefully sipping on a glass of bubbly, looking up at the stars glowing above her. She thought about all the people that she missed the most. "Well the pleasure party starts in ten minutes fellas, so if you wanna sit in, just let me tell you right now it's going to be one hell of a showcase! Success said just too damned juiced. "Babe you know where imma be at . . . . Chow!" Lollipop said . . . And then they were gone. Nesto didn't care for the toys and shit, that they were about to display, plus there was a good chance he would get a chance to break' em all in on his next visit to lollipops house. The thought alone of just sitting in there getting exhibited sexual toys made him stray away from attending. He felt that women should stick to attending that type of stuff and just surprise him. "So what brings you boys all the way to the other side of the states" one of the haitian dreadz asked. These two niggas looked like they were "wit da shit" so Nesto decided to gas them up a little bit. "Well actually, we were looking for a connect that could hook us up with the man" Nesto said with a serious look. "Yea, da snow man" Finesse followed, with a little bit of humor but serious as fuck. "Is dat right the other dread said, as he twirled around on his feet and handed his cane to his buddy. "What are you looking for? Snow? Peruvian? Blow? White girl? The haitian was damn near levitating at this point when he just thought about drugs. He acted like he just got a nut off or something. "Im your man! "Whoo doo yaa tink make all deese nice tings possibo?" The dread said with his haitian slurr. "We already getting our work for the low" Nesto said "yea, what can you do for us" Finesse added making them sound like hot commodities. "Da low?" Dread said confused. "What de ell iz dat?" He questioned. "Well we pretty much get it for a cheap price now" Nesto said cuttin it dry. "And want to know . . . How we can get it from you for better" Finesse stated with a serious look. Dread placed his pointer finger on his temple, then took a minute to respond. "I can't promise dat me can beat da price, but what me can promise is dat it be bout ten times pure dan de garbage dat chu gettin righ now" he said leaning back in his chair, confident in the work he was holding. "Me name is jahsun! And what bout chu?" He questioned attempting to get a formal introduction. "This is Nesto and im Finesse!" Finesse said gaining entry on the conversation. "We already getting them for 17 flat . . . So what can you do for us?" Nesto asked trying to pull his fishing line in. "Me might can get dem to you fo 16.5 Da lowest me will go. You gettn dat bumaclod bullchit and das why it be so cheap" jah said. "Me coke can be hit one time an still be 10 time mo betta den the chit you got, you hear?" Jah added, now a little annoyed. He then sent his man on another ten minute run; his man came back with a white and grey gucci backpack. When he floored the zipper, he removed 1 kilo of cocaine "100% grade a" jah said, as he slit the pack open with a fancy butterfly knife. He put some coke on the plate and handed Nesto and ness two straws . . . "Enjoy dis" he said. Nesto had watched too many gangster flicks to know that this was not the time to retire his jet ski's . . . Jah was trying to test them to see if they were narc's. Nesto reached in his pocket and pulled out his california driver's license. He slid a bump of the powder from the plate and placed it on his hand between the thumb and index finger before he took a whiff. When he inhaled, he instantly got a drain that ran all the way to the back of his throat. "It's good" Nesto confirmed pinching his nose and shaking his head slightly from side to side. He then passed the plate to Nesse. Ness took the card from Nesto and indulged in on the session as well. After Finesse got his drain he passed the plate back and said "yea . . . It's good!" From that point, they knew they had just met the investors for operation "gmb".

"Now lets get down to business" he said as he paced around grabbing the hair on his chin, with one hand behind his back like he was on straight mack status or sumthin. "Me wan to elp you" he said. "Since u girl iz de frien of me wife" he said. "But that aint my girl" Nesto said trying to cut it short. "Well whoeva she be to you boy, you don't even know when you got a good one!" Jah said shaking his head and sounding frustrated. "Let jus put it like dis" jah said, as he stopped every movement and put his serious face on.

"If you buy dis from me . . . . You buys five at a time, no less . . . Down digg?" Jah said slurring his words in haitian. "Ag-in, 80,000 no ting less, can you cali boys andle dat? Nesto and ness held their shit as they nodded in agreeance. "Now listen dis here . . ." Dreadz said and paused. "Me am goin front you da first five . . . . "But!!" He emphasized, "you deal wit me and me only." He added "any-ting else will be in completely diss-respect. We no need no extra problems in da circle, right fellas?" Jah positioned his self for the arrival of the answer to his question. "We got chu "Nesto confirmed, so excited inside that he almost busted a nut, as his hands began to itch. Finesse felt he was either feeling his booger Candy or just couldn't believe what the fuck was happening. Maybe a little of both because Nesto had that same feeling. "Do chu gota mule?" Jah said referring to a runner. "Yea" Nesto said "good!" He added and gave Nesto a very powerful handshake that spoke tremendous volumes. "Man, truss an kno tings like dis don appen ev'ry day." Jah said. He told Nesto that his mule could get past the mexican border, which was the meeting spot, but after that, they would be on their own. It was more than halfway, so they wouldn't have complained, if he would have said texas. "Ay jah normally I don't do this front shit, but we really need this shit right now . . . so as long as you keep us taken care of . . . . We gone make sure that the money's right . . . Aight!! Nesto said, as he began to feel his self rhyming and shit. "Like me say "jah started "you take care of I . . . . Me take care of you, it go two ways" . . . by the time they were finished wrapping up business, they had time to smoke a couple more sticks before the girls came back. Jah told them that the mule would meet them for the first run about three days after they made it back to cali, they all agreed. When Lollipop and raisun returned to the back, they had all types of goodies and shit. They both were smiling like they just visited santa. After they all mingled for about another hour, they left. When they got back to the strip, Nesto told Lollipop that he just wanted to get back to the room and chill. It had been a long night and they had a whole lot to think about. This shit had just got real, and it definitely was no looking back now. Nesto thought about how crazy it was because he was only 13 when he got introduced to the game. When he got out of school for the day, he would sneak up to the block where all the d-boys and game-players were hangin out. They were who he looked up to back then. It was natural for him to want to be just like them and have a lot of money one day. He figured now was time to proceed with his life and live! . . . Live out that dream that been treading water in the back of his mind. Nesto realized that him and Finesse was ready to play chess now, they had all the pieces they would need, and as long as they were the ones moving the pieces, they could always pick up new pieces to put on the board, if need be!

CHP 14
TOO MANY CHIEFS AND NOT ENOUGH INDIANS

Finesse and Nesto woke up the next day with two days left in Miami until they hit the runway back to the sunshine state. Shit they had only been there for five days and were already up to 160 Stacks cold cash. Not to mention all the expensive jewelry, and a whole bunch of clothes that they had payed top dollar for. They tore up Miami for the next two days like a occupy Oakland demonstration, and on the last day before they left, Lollipop said that she wanted to take everybody to this one club "karu &y" somewhere off N.W. 14th St. They had seen the nightlife on southbeach alive in full effect, and they would have never thought that there was another little movement jumping off right in Miami's downtown district right off the famous causeway. The club had opened up in 2006 and already had a name foe itself from all the stars like mary j. Blige, christina milian, keri hilson, and not to mention fat joe's video "I won't tell" was also shot there. They were having so much fun. They were parting like rockstarz, Miami would definately catch a glimpse of Nesse and Nesto again. By the time they got back to Oakland, CA they had divided up the money and they all had 52 Stacks a piece. Shit raisun had just so happen to get drug along and now she was sitting on thousands that fast! They say if you hang around five rich muthafuckaz that you will be the sixth and this was a perfect example of that. "Girl thank you for making me apart of your trip" raisun said to Lollipop. After they blew threw a couple of lights coming up 98ᵗʰ, they bent a couple more corners to drop Lollipop off. "Girl it ain't nothin, we do shit like this all the time, you were actually right on time because my girlfriend was gonna come but she couldn't make it" Lollipop said as they pulled up in front of her house and parked for a min. "You should ask Nesto to bring you by sometime, it really goes down over here!" Lollipop said wishing she could get raisun over there and reek some benefits. "I don't think so!" Nesse said giving Lollipop a funny look. "We know how you rockn! He added full of humor. "Boy shut up! . . . . Hater!" Lollipop shot back! "Bye you guys!" She said as she was getting out of Nesse's coupe. "And Nesto can you please come see me Daddy, so all these good toys I bought don't go to waste" Lollipop whined" aight" he assured her "imma have to call you later and make me a appointment" Nesto said gassing her up. After she grabbed all the bags that belonged to her including the bag full of money, she was gone. When Nesto and Finesse left lollipops they slid by the house to drop everything off including raisun. They were finally back inside their four corners and Nesto & Nesse had some corner cuttin to do. By the time they got to west Oakland they seen some new cats holdin post where they usually met up with Stacks. They slid up . . ." Ayy you seen Stackz?" Nesto inquired as they tried to locate his whereabouts. "Na" the youngin said "Stackz ain't been out here all day!" He added "let me call this nigga!" Nesto said as he whipped his phone out. It rang and it rang. Ring! Ring! No answer. This was totally not like Stackz at all. They called a couple more times to see if he would answer. No luck. Something was wrong. They hit a couple of spots where they knew Stackz liked to hang out at. They rolled through cypress, the lower bottoms, and campbell village and still no luck wit Stackz.

As Lollipop put her key in the door and turned the lock, she got rushed from the back by a pack of goonz. "Welcome home bitch" one of them said as he hit her with the butt of the gun. Lollipop dropped to the ground "what do you want?" She said frantically. "The money! Where's the money?" One of the goonz said as he stood over her. "What money?" She asked dumbfoundedly. Bam!, Bam! . . . . The goon was going to work on her face, while the other men that came with him ran through the house rummaging looking for money and valuables. "You punk muthafuckaz, broke ass nigg-" . . . . And before she could finish the sentence blam! . . . . Blam! . . . . Blam! The repititions of blows would not stop as the man continued to beat the life out of Lollipop. Blam! . . . . Blam! Lollipops vision came to a blurr as she started to black out. One of the mens phone rang, but would not get a response. "Nuthin!" One of them said as he ran back down the stairs empty handed. The one that beat her senselessly rummaged through the shopping bags. "Bingo!" He said as he opened the bag that contained the money she had just brought back from Miami. "What money huh?" He said as he gave her another blow to the head that put her lights out. "Ahy yall niggaz take what you can find, tie this bitch up and put her in a trash bag, and get rid of her." The goonz finished running through the house taking any valuables they seen from electronics to jewelry and furs. When they got ready to leave, they let the whole clip of the semi-automatic pistol rip the flesh off her body and then put her in a trash bag and dragged her outside to the trunk.

When Nesse and Nesto got finished riding around they went back to the house so they could finish unpacking all their things. "Man out of all the trips I done took . . . . That had to take the cake!" Nesse announced as he dumped all the money on the floor. "This was trappin at it's finest." Nesto thought to himself. They went from some niggas fresh out from rita's house to sittn sky high. Nesto planned on doing something nice for Lollipop tonight. After all the hustlin they had just did, Nesto knew for a fact that them bandz would make her dance! When they finished taking care of their business, Nesto figured he'd swing by to show her some appreciation wit his magic stick. Fifteen minutes later they finally got the call from Stacks "what's poppin my niggas" he said "I heard yall rolled through lookin for me" he added "yea me and Nesse just got back and we were coming through to check the trap" Nesto said as he checked his watch, debating if he still wanted to slide back through there. "Well im out here if you need me dogg!" Stackz said. "It's going to be another couple of days before we touch down on dat work too, so you just gotta be patient. We gotta new line wit some even better shit so just hold out." Nesto said. "True!" Stackz said "so gimme a couple of days, you just lay low aight and its gon be good." Nesto assured him. Man the whole team was about to eat. Nesto had planned to fuck with jah-sun for about a solid year on da work and then he could start makin his exit. Only the greedy muthafuckaz faithfully reaked te benefits of having no success in whatever it was they did. Greed for money could keep anyone running back to the game because of the people that they dealt with applying constant pressure to keep things going to help them get by and pay their bills. Sometimes the bottom line was it was hard to cut the relationship with the fast cash. After Nesto and Nesse finished getting unpacked raisun and her two lil sisters came over to keep them company. Raisun said that she wanted to come over and do something special to show how grateful she was to be apart of the escapade and all-star weekend. "Wassup yall?" She said as the door swung open like she lived there. "Wassup babe?" Nesse said. "Sup yall" jamaica said as she slid past raisun. "Hey" shawna said as she filled in behind jamaica. "Wish I coulda got a chance to go to Miami" she said smilin and rollin her eyes at the same dam time lookn at raisun. "So we brought fish&chips, shrimp, salmon, and lobster tails" jamaica said tryin to get the jump off started. "Damn all dat money yall got and yall niggas ain't got no furniture?" Jamaica said joking. "As a matter of fact . . . ." Nesto said thinking about "naughty nadia" that he had met at the fast food joint across the street. He decided to call her and see what was up. She told him she had a busy week coming up and that she was on her way to vegas in recognition for a nomination in this years 2010 avn show in las vegas, nevada. They talked for a good while and did some catching up on each other and what they had missed. Nadia told Finesse that she would call him and try to hook up on the next weekend but she couldn't make any promises. "Kool" he said and hung up. By that time jamaica and shawna had just finished cookin up all the food. It smelled good as hell. Everybody grabbed a plate and was ready to eat. They flipped on the news to find out whats been going on in the world, and their mouths dropped as they all witnessed the first story of the night. Nesto, raisun, and Nesse looked at each other as if they couldn't believe what they saw.

CHP 15
"THE BEGINNING
OF THE END"

"This is faith fancher reporting live from East Oakland. I'm at the scene of a brutal homicide that was said to have taken place just hours ago. Police say they believe that it may have been a robbery. It all started tonight when the neighbors next to this house here behind me made a 911 call to an emergency operator to report an explosion. Upon arrival, Oakland police officers found the body identified as 26 yr old Lola stevenson in the trunk of this mercedes benz cl500 that had been set on fire right here in the driveway of her home. The police have no clues at this time, and crime stoppers is offering a 50,000 reward for anybody with any informatiion leading to the arrest and conviction of anyone involved. This is faith fancher reporting live from Oakland" the reporter said as they ran the first story of the night. They all sat in the living room in total amazement not believing it at all. Nesto had felt that someone had just tooken something close to him and he didn't know how to feel. He was sick, and angry, and confused and just wanted to make someone pay.

Surely as soon as Nesto found out who that someone was they would have a high price to pay. He just sat there not being able to control the emotions that came over him. Raisun and Nesse tried to comfort him but it just wasn't working. "That just don't make no sense at all" raisun said as jamaica and shawna sat there puzzled. "Yall know her?" Shawna said. "Yea girl thats who we just took a trip with" Lollipop said as she started to fill her sisters in on what was going on. "I need to take a ride" Nesto said as he grabbed his coat and left. He needed to go and see for himself if this was all real. He did about a hundred in the third lane trying to get to the 98th ave exit. When he pulled up in front of lollipops, he seen the tow truck taking the benz away all burnt up to a crisp "fuck!!" He screamed as a tear drop rolled down his face "I didn't even get a chance to say goodbye" he thought to himself. Whoever did this had to be watching her and knew exactly when she was coming back. "Damn baby . . . . If you can only hear me, I just wanna tell you . . . . We was a good look together and im sorry that I didn't get a chance to tell you this in person but . . . . I love you!!. I'm thankful for every opportunity that you dropped in my lap to help me better my situation. Please god take care of my girl and accept her into your kingdom, she had a good heart." Nesto never thought in a million years something like this would happen. That justgoes to show that you can be here one day . . . . And gone the next, so make the most out of today.

There was a drug trade going on, on the other side of town. A black ss pulled into acorn plaza on the side of mcdonalds to meet a young head. There was a beat up box chevy that pulled right in next to the black ss. "Spank" was the name of the man that sat at the wheel of the chevy. He was a new head that had just jumped off the porch and was trying to make a name for himself as a jacker on the streetz of Oakland. Word was that he had ten under his belt and was lookin for eleven for the right price. "Rook" was the driver of the ss. He was some new nigga dat had just moved to the area since that hurricane katrina shit. Word was out that he was just trying to pick his life back up since he left everything back home. Rook was a small time nigga who was just moving a kick at a time, and was known for steppn on niggas toes. For some reason he was still squirmin around on these streeetz. They say that he came up off of robbin major factors, but alot of the players that he had robbed had his name in their mouth and it was only a matter of time before his lifestyle caught up with him. "What up nigga?" Spank said as he bounced inside of the black super sport. "How many?" Spank said keeping it business. "Just one" rook said pulling a see through plastic bag full of wrapped up hundred dollar bills out of his boxers. "How much is this?" Spank asked "20 grand, all crispy hunnids" rook said anxiously ready to get his hands on his first key ever. "Aight hit me!" Spank said as he gave rook a pound with his fist. "Bet!" Rook said as he was getting out of the car. The ss pulled away and exited acorn plaza, then sped off down the street towards lowell middle school. Rook hopped back in the car and gave his commander in charge a call. "Hey" he said when the other end of the line picked up. "Wassup?" The voice from the other end replied. "Touchdown!" Rook announced. "Good . . . . Good!" The voice replied.

As soon as Nesto got his self together he drove down to lake merrit so he could get his mind together. He walked around a couple of times and found women and men but mostly women gettin laps in tryin to keep their shape up. The lights that hung over the water made it look truly beautiful at night, but in the daytime it looked like the same water that bewildered wild creatures like swamp thing. Nesto was still puzzled about the whole Lollipop thing. Any other time it would be a million people at her house that didn't know when to leave. Now all of a sudden she ends up in the trunk of her own car on fire and nobody saw anything. That was some real bullshit and it was tearing Nesto up thinkn about it. The coldest part about it is that there were so many people that Lollipop was dealing with that he personally did not know where to start. He would have to play it by ear, because whoever it was would not make it to see the new year. Shit, it was the least he could do.

CHP 16
"FLOWERZ"

After a whole week of preparation for lollipops funeral Nesto finally got everything together. He payed for the whole funeral by himself with no help. Nesse told Nesto that he had something to do with his money. He had been actn kinda brand new lately. On sunday the day of lollipops funeral the place was packed to the capacity with friends and family. Nesto sat on the front row with Nesse and raisun, and the few people that were present in Lollipop's immediate family. Even jah-sun and success came down to pay their respects for their friend as he mourned. Success really took it hard. Lollipop's casket never opened to expose her immflammed body. There was every kind of flower, every color, with a different scent. Nesto showed a slideshow with every photo that they could find of her, and gave away t-shirts that said "we love you & gone but not forgottten" it was a sad day. Her funeral was wrapped up with stevie wonders "ribbon in the sky" they released a dove into the air after everybody piled out of C.P. Bannon, and then headed to rollin hills, so she could be buried next to her mother. When they were finished there, Nesto and Finesse had raisun and jamaica fry up some fish and a couple other little appetizers at the house for any of the family and friends who wanted to come by and mourn with them for the homegoing of Lollipop.

CHP 17
INTENT TO DISTRIBUTE

"Hello" platinum said as she answered her phone trying to figure out the caller with the blocked I.D "wasup baby?" Finesse said. "Who dis?" She said puzzled. "You must give your number away alot" Nesse said "man wassup? Platinum said relieved, you da one been actin like you too good to pick up a phone and say hi. I ain't seen or heard from you since the night you came over." Platinum said with defense. "Damn u sound like u really miss a nigga" Finesse said trying to put some humor back into the situation at hand. "No, I miss him though" she said referring to the manpower that he had in his pants. "Hey look im on my way to your house, so get dressed . . . . I need you to take a ride with me." Finesse said trying to rush her off the line. "Ride wit you where?" She said "just wait and see" he said. And just like that he hung up. After about two hours had passed they were in route to new mexico, and since time don't wait for no man they had a sense of urgency about gettin there. Platinum was driving ness's coupe and him and Nesto were tailing them to make sure everything went as planned. They called jah-sun to let him know that they were on the way. He informed them that his mule was already halfway there to them. Finesse had told platinum that this was probably the easiest money that she would ever make. They stopped at some run down motel on the side of the road on their way back to get some sleep. Platinum had to call in for work the next day, but what they were paying her was the equivalence of about four of her checks from work put together. Nesto and Nesse made it worth her wild considering the risk that she was taking smuggling these drugs back to cali for them, so they gave her 2500 for doing the pick up (a stack on the way, and 1500 more dollars when they returned). When they got back, they had five kilos of peruvian white that they were ready to distribute. They had the best coke on this side of california and it was just a matter of time before all the fiends found out about it. They were neatly wrapped with a stamp of a black dragon on top. Nesto called Stackz to let him know that the light was on, and that he would be comin through the first thing in the morning to drop him off the work. Nesto slid through the high rises to drop Stackz off the work and pick up the money from the last run. Shit was going sweet. They finally had the money flowing in and a solid connect that was going to put that 401k in effect. They ran this same pattern for the next couple of months everybody was eatin now. Stackz was doing his thang. His turnover rate was so fast that they had got up to moving 3 kicks a day, not to mention the pillz and weed that was flying away as well. They started spreading the coke out all over the place. They flooded the whole east side especially the 80's all the way to 106th ave. Everybody that had any type of real money was buyin from them. Ja-sun was so happy to be seeing a pretty penny again that he knocked another 500 off of the price that they were coppin at for staying loyal and true to the game. Two months after that Nesto and Nesse were back at the auction to talk to frank. They put a down payment on two houses and came back the next week with the rest of the money in cash. It wasn't hard to figure out that they were bringing in 680,400 a week and just about three million dollars a month. This was the life. Platinum ended up quitting her job and began picking up work full time as a nine to five. They even put Moco to work. She was so tired of dealing with the people at da bank, that her and platinum instantly got close, and together they became the mules that made everything move. One was headz and and the other was tailz. Just in case they were to ever get knocked the rollerz would never get both . . . . The coke and the money. After frank had his money they exchanged the little flat on fruitvale for two beautiful houses, one in union city and the other one in hayward. All the moving around they did, shit they never were there anywayz. Nesto instantly got his baby momma and the kids up out of the hood and let them stay there. Finesse moved raisun and her lil sister in with him. They had become so much like family. They did everything together with them. The last trip they had took was to the dominican republics newest luxury resort which had offered the ultmate escape to paradise. From the heart stoppping mountain biking through the twenty-seven waterfalls of damajagua to adrenaline pumping river rafting through the "dominican alps" they enjoyed the four night accomidation with roundtrip V.I.P airport transportation not to mention the $250 towards treatments and services at the extensive spa and wine tasting gallery. They really learned how to spend money. Nesto and his kids had the time of their life. It was truly quality time. He was finally starting to feel like the man he knew was inside of him. Along with the rest of the people they began to run into Nesse and Nesto were now carrying all family and friends on their backs. Two weeks after that they were back to see frank again. This time Finesse left with a porsce 911 carrera 4s which was a rear engine, 4 wheel drive, 2 passenger, 2 door coupe, dual overhead cam, 24 valve flat 6 aluminum heads, and direct fuel injection. 0-60 In four seconds with a top speed of 185 mph appraised at 93,000. Nesto picked up one of those new cadillac escalade hybrids wit front engine, rear wheel drive, 8 passenger, 5 doors, 16 valves,6.0 Liters v-8, 332 horsepower, continously variable automatic with four fixed ratios and manumatic shifting. Shit was serious. After a while it wasn't hard to figure out who was touching their dope on the streetz, shit you could tell by type of whip the d-boys were in and could tell that it was a good chance that they didn't fall too far from the tree. Nesto and Nesse even started to wear the clothes that rich people wanted; cardigian sweaters by louis vuitton, v necks by polo, pants by marc jacob, shoes by prada. And sunglasses by sean john. Well atleast this summed up their outfits for the day. Nesto and Nesse no doubt had some big thangs going on. They hit up all the raiders games, even though they lost damn near every one, they were still die hard fans. They partied with the dragons motorcycle club and just about every other reputable biker club including the wise guys, breaking bread, and the kings of cali. For about a year straight there never was hardly a dull moment.

CHP 18
"FOUL PLAY"

Ring! Ring!, Ring! Ring!! Nestos phone rang as Nesto layed sprawled out after a long night with naughty nadia. They had been hangin out alot lately. "Hello?" **Click!** The first call he figured that he must of lost the call. When he got the other call . . . . And another call . . . . **Ring! . . . Ring!** . . . . And when Nesto finally did pick up the phone again . . . . **Click!** Somebody was really playin on the phone and had nothing else better to do. **Ring!** . . . . **Ring!** . . . Fed up from all the bullshit Nesto answered the phone with a mouth full to say "ay yo look yo bitch ass ain't got nuthin else better to do than to play on the phone this early in the morning?" When he got ready to hang it up the last time he heard somebody speak "it's me dawg, whats wrong?" It was Nesse. "Wassup man! Why you playin on the phone like dat? Nesto said. "What you talkin about? This my first time callin." Finesse said. Well somebody playin on my phone, because they been blowin up my phone all morning and when I answer the phone they hang up, Nesto told him. The other line beeped. After he debated to himself whether to answer the call or not, something told him to answer the phone. "Wassup pussy?"

Said the caller on the other end of the telephone. "Who the fuck is this?" Nesto growled "this ya worst nightmare, so listen up you fuck nigga. It's a new rank out here and you ain't on top no more, so you and yo boy need to bow out gracefully or get swept. Thats if you wanna live! Pussy! . . . . Haaaaaggggh!!" The caller laughed rediicously with no punch line. "Ay whoever this is you ain't ready for my team nigga! Be safe! I mean dat! . . . . Play wit fire and you gon get blazed! Bitch! Nesto said. **Click!** And he hung up the phone. Somebody was seriously gettin besides theirself **ring!** . . . . **Ring!** . . . . **Ring!** . . . . **Ring!** After the madness, Nesto didn't even answer the phone anymore. He let it go straight to voicemail and continued with his conversation that he was having with Nesse. "Yea man somebody really playin now" Nesto told him. "Who was it?" Nesse said anxiously after Nesto clicked back over. "Shit I have no idea, but whoever it is talkin bout bowing out gracefully or get swept" . . . . "What?" Nesse yelled across the phone angrily "yea talkin bout there's a new rank out here. Nesto said as he filled him in. "Ay niggas is crazy if they think they can fuck wit us Nesse, I swear im mobbin" Finesse said.

Somewhere in the confines of secracy the D.E.A. Were investigating and making preparations for the prosecution of major players that were taking part in the distribution of controlled substances at interstate and international levels after recieving numerous annonymous phone calls. Thr investigation for the prosecution of criminals and drug gangs who perputrated violence in the community and terrorized citizens through fear and intimidation had become another topic for them which brought out their special gang task force unit. After recieving this assignment they were officially on one to keep management of a national drug intelligence program in cooperation with federal, state, local, and foreign officials to collect, analyze, and disseminate strategic and operational drug intelligence information.

When Nesto finally did listen to the the stalking voicemail, he heard the same voice of the caller that had interupted his phone call with Nesse earlier. "Watch the news pussy!".

"Ring! . . . . **Ring!** . . . . **Ring!** . . . . **Ring!**

Nesto picked up the phone to find a collect call from dinosaur. "You have a collect call from an inmate at the alameda county sherriffs department, to accept this call now press 4 or hang up!" The operator said. Nesto hit the number four on the phone to find dinosaur upset and hysterical "bruh somebody snitchin!" He yelled "they droppin dimes around this muthafucka im tellin you, they knew where all the work was at, all the money . . . Everything. It's bad dog!" Dinosaur was losing it frantically. "Relax, imma send somebody for you just be kool." Nesto said trying to calm him down. "I can't calm down dog, I'm on parole and I got no bail, im stuck! . . . **Fuck!** . . . And my lil cutey-poo birthday tomorrow! He said. "Don;t worry about that I got you" Nesto said "listen imma send somebody down there . . . . You know I don't trust these phones . . . . Be easy!" And just like that Nesto hung up the phone. As he pushed end on the phone Nesto threw his phone against the wall and watched it shatter to pieces. **"Fuck!"** He said "I definately don't need any ties to the feds" he thought to himself. They probably already had the line tapped, and he was willing to bet on it. It was obviously time for a new phone. Nesse and Nesto's game of chess had gotten interesting. The wolves were definately preying on their ponds and if they didn't get a grip fast they would witness a checkmate!!!

CHP 19
"CHECK"

Achevy with four men inside pulled up to a house known for heavy drug trafficking. As they loaded up their assault rifles and ski masks, they let the crowd of teenagers ride past on their custom made scraper bikes with they're built in stereo systems that made them sound like a marching band. Inside the house there were 2 men going to work on a video game which had their full attention. There were two more men downstairs. The two at the table were getting ready to bust a couple of keys down to ounces, while the other four men were upstairs. Two of the men were running the cash through an electronic money machine while the other two were holdin post with ak-47's. The two guys that were holdin post were arguin over who could handle the high power rifles the best. After the door to the house got kicked in and off the hinges, neither men would ever know just how true their statements was. All you could hear was a chatter of gunplay. When the men wearing the ski masks seen the feet running down the stairs they redirected their weapons and went to work on them. They never had a chance. After the two men counting the money seen their soldiers drop, one grabbed a mac and slapped the dick in and hid in the closet. The other one jumped up to get his heat he had sitting on the table but never made it as the first man with the ski mask ran upstairs choppin away tearing chunks out of his body as he tried to put the whole clip in him. The other guy that was countin the money jumped out of the closet likle max payne firing shots at the ski mask that stood right in front of him and hit him right in the chest, while the other ski mask ran upstairs and finished him off letting his chopper go to work until he felt satisfied. The other two ski masks entered the house after doing a full search around the perimeter for any extra knuckleheads that were hangin around, after they didn't find anyone they entered the house to see the men that were already hit. One was still alive and crawling for the door before they finished him off and sent any hope for survival straight to hell. After searching the whole flat, they finally found what they were looking for . . . . **Coke and money**. After escaping out the house with all the work(ten keys) and about twenty-five Stacks they got back into the chevy and sped away. "Im shot!" The passenger yelled out frantically as he seen the blood gushing out of the left side of his chest. "You are huh?" The driver said as he reached in his waistband for the.40 Caliber he had stashed on his hip. **Boom! . . . Boom! . . . Boom!!** As he sent the brains of the passenger straight out the window. He reached over his lifeless body and opened the passenger door then pushed him out of the car in the broad daylight. "Only the strong survive baby! And before the weak leave a trail, they die!" He said laughing as if it was the funniest thing that he had seen all day.

After Nesto finished getting a couple of bags packed he sent nadia down to the station to see what was going on with dyno. He gave her about a stack to go and put on his boy's books along with the keys to the camarro ss. The rest would have to come in money order, because it was too hot. It turned out that they had dinosaur booked under the rico act, conspiracy to distribute cocaine and other uncontrolled substances. When he was packed up and ready to go he hopped in the escalade to give it the first run ever since he had brought it home. He needed to find out where Nesse was but he had no phone. "I wonder if he's tried to call me" Nesto thought to himself. From there he drove to the sprint store to switch his phone number to a new phone. He figured if he was going to get a completely new phone then he might as well get a whole new service provider so he went with sprint. He bought two phones, one for himself and the other one for Nesse.

After leaving the station nadia pulled up to the light at the intersection. When she checked the rearview she seen a black lexus coupe sc430 pull up right behind her, then on the side of her as if it was going to play chicken with traffic facing the opposite direction. When nadia got a clear view of the driver it was raisun, and she had remembered her from las palmas the one day talking to Nesto. Nadia rolled down the window to see what she wanted. When she got greeted with the barrel of raisuns 380 "checkmate bitch" raisun hollered. Nadia frantically panicked reaching under Nesto's seat for some protection when she found the nine-millimeter. **Pop!** . . . **Pop!**

Agents moved in on finesses house waiting for the signal to carry out the raid that had been ordered by the federal bureau of investigations. Feds assisted with the D.E.A. surrounded the house with their weapons drawn. After an unannounced entry and aggressive search of the house they found Nesse in the attic hiding under a pile of clothes. Nesse had seen the agents surrounding his house from the surveillance monitor that was connected to his television. "Freeze mutherfucker!" It didn't take long before his whole world came crashing down.

CHP 20
"AINT NO LOVE"

Drug enforcement agent mchenry had Nesse in the interrogation room beating the shit out of him . . . "Your a cold piece of work" mchenry said as he climbed up into finesses face. "Does your boy know your a piece of shit yet?" Mchenry said highly upset. "Fuck you!" Finesse roared at mchenry at the top of his lungs. "You wanna be the man don't you?" Mchenry said drilling him. "Do you hear me talking to you? . . . . No?" Mchenry said as he reached out and slapped the spit out of nesses mouth. "You know you got people out here dying for no reason?" **Pow!** Mchenry gave Finesse a stiff one to the jawbone and then rolled his sleeve up. "You don't have a god damn thing to say huh? Mchenry said climbing back in finesses's face almost standin on Finesse's lap while he was cuffed to the chair. "Piece of shit!" Mchenry shouted as he became more and more agitated with finesses's non chalantness. Nesto had called Nesse about a thousand times and got no answer. "What the fuck?" He thought. He then called nadia . . . No answer! Nesto couldn't get in contact with anybody. This was not the time to start loosing communication. Nesto had all the money packed up that he pulled out from several of his savings accounts. It was approximately 2.5 Million sitting in the back of nestos truck and he just couldn't figure out for the life of him his next move. Not to mention all the bricks he still had floating around in the streets. Nesto planned to go and get all the work that was still in the traphouses that hadn't been hit yet. Little did he know he was hangin on a string by visiting each of the stash spots just barely beating the agents by minutes. When he got to each house, he got what he needed and left. When Nesto got to the last stash house he was puzzled when he seen some rashy ass youngsta dragging garbage bags out of his trap house to a dirty box chev. Nesto felt on the floor for a russian A.K that he had bought for days like this, which hadn't been too many. When he put the brakes on, the door swung open and he was on the concrete all in the matter of seconds. "What the fuck do you think your doing?" Nesto said curiously trying to get to the bottom of who the hell this guy was. "What it look like?" The rashy youngsta said still comin full force trying to draw his weapon from his waistband **clack! Clack!** The russian A.K spit two 223's from the semi and leg checked the street punk. "Wait!" He said "don't kill me" spank pleaded as he hit the ground. "Who the fuck sent you to my stash house in the first place?" Nesto asked in purte curiousity. "Tell me and I **might** let you live. Nesto said putting the emphasis on might. "Stackz!, ... Stackz man, he paid me a nice piece of change to robb all the stash houses and take the dope and money" spank said, spilling his guts. All of a sudden there was a shower of broken glass flying up from behind him. Nesto pulled spank up by his neck dragging him for cover until he made it to the door of the flat. "What else" Nesto said as he made us call the cops and give em all the locations, so your empire would fall, then we could emerge with his. Everything was planned the whole time." Spank said "I got my first job when we killed the girl and put her in da trunk." Spank added ready to tell everything in exchange for his life.

"So tell me was being the right hand man not good enough for you or what?" Agent mchenry said trying to get some answers out of Nesse. "Your going to do alot of time you piece of shit" he assured Finesse as he gave him another blow to the face. "Suck my dick, you fuckin pig, you aint got shit on me "Nesse said full of confidence. "**First of all** . . . . Where your going im pretty sure somebody else will take you up on that offer . . . . **2nd** . . . . We got everything on you from the hit you ordered on Lola stevenson to all your conversations orchestrating drug trades from Oakland to new mexico." The agent said. "Your fucked" he re-assured him.

Nesto had killed three of the agents in a fight for his life. "What the fuck you say" Nesto said looking down at spank not believing his ears "you fuckin liar" Nesto said still in total amaze of everything he was hearing. "No im not lying" spank said crying. "Put yur weapon down now!" The agents demanded from the bullhorns. "I can't do that!" Nesto yelled back. "What else?" He screamed at the young thug as he dodged more bullets that ricocheted right past his head. "Man yo boy wanted yo spot! . . . . So he put us all on the payroll before yall came back from Miami. Nesse told us that you wasn't gone pay us what we were worth and that he would double our pay if we came to work for him. Everything was all planned from the jump, from him meeting raisun before yall took the trip . . . to me and Stackz going to rob and kill Lollipop".

"What?" Not Stackz Nesto thought. After I had put this nigga up wit some cash too? . . . He gone play me? "Nesto started ramblin off losing one half of his mind. Nesto had heard enough, he switched the semi automatic rifle to fully and put a whole round in spanks head. "Now who's da pussy" Nesto said as he popped in another hundred round dick and ran from out of the doorway still draggin spanks now dead body across the grass for cover while he attempted to make his way back to the truck. Nesto let the russian A.K dance around knockin all the agents down that popped up like target practice on duck hunt. When he got back to the truck he threw spanks lifeless body to the ground and gave it a mouthful of spit before he threw it in drive and hit every back street he knew to evade the rest of the agents that were persistently trying to assist in his assasination. As Nesto bent corner after corner, he flashbacked to all the priceless moments he had spent wit his boy Nesse. Everything that he had ever wanted for his self, he wanted for his boy as well . . . . And this is how he re-pays me?" Nesto said to himself.

"I hope you rott in that little sardine can we're going to put you in." I hope somebody fucks your little pretty black ass until it looks like chewed up bubble gum" agent mchenry said furiously. Deep down he knew really that what they had on him would not keep him down long at all. They were scared to waste anymore time so they had to move when they did before he decided to take a trip.

Nesto entered the freeway. The showers of bullets paraded right through every window that his truck had. Bulletproof windows definately would have not been a bad investment. He looked at the agents that raced next to him, then up at the rigg carrying the gasoline that rode right next to them. Nesto swung the chopper across his chest with one hand on the wheel and put the gun out the window and started to fire recklessly at the tanker as he speeded up.

After mchenry got tired of beating the life out of Nesse, he drug him to a vacated cell. "Here's your snitch!" Mchenry said as he dragged Nesse into the cell wit dinosaur and threw a rusty dagger to the floor. "Snitches get stitches right?" He said laughing as he left Nesse in there to fend for his life.

By the time Nesto got to the edwards exit he got off the freeway. As soon as he hit the hill he just start throwin money right out the window. He had so much that the few couple hundred thousand wouldn't hurt him," shit these streetz deserved it" he thought to himself. After he made it rain all the way down 73rd. He got olled right over the ramp blew past the coliseum and headed towards the airport. He thought to himself about Lollipop . . . . And how Stackz would have to pay . . . . How Finesse would have to suffer . . . . And how it was a matter of time before they had to cross paths again. Jealousy and envy made enemies . . . . Aint no love in this town!

To be continued